Sally stood rooted to the spot, gazing at him in disbelief, until he was standing before her and those familiar periwinkle-blue eyes set in a tanned open face held hers in total amazement. The babble in the hall seemed to recede, and for a few minutes it was as if there were just the two of them alone together.

'Oh, my God—it's Sally—Sally Lawson,' Jack said softly.

He had a lovely voice—deep and warm—and it brought all sorts of memories tumbling back through Sally's mind—quite unsuitable memories... The first time Jack kissed her, the feel of his body against hers when they danced, the first time they'd…

She swallowed hard—she was damned if she was going to go overboard welcoming Dr Jack McLennan!

Dear Reader

Friends Reunited, school reunions…all places where we are deliberately seeking to contact people we used to know, and to discover how their life has panned out over the years. Thinking about this made me wonder what would happen if you were a single girl and had a completely chance meeting with an old love from many years before. I envisaged my heroine experiencing just that, and it triggering a life-change that she could never have dreamed of! What will her reaction be when her old flame turns up out of the blue? How will they have changed? What will their feelings be about each other?

Let's face it: wouldn't we all be curious to know how we'd regard someone we used to be head over heels in love with and then unexpectedly met again, and intrigued to know how his life had fared without us? In Sally's case, it shows her what true love really feels like!

I do so hope you enjoy reading about Sally and Jack as much as I had fun writing their story.

Best wishes

Judy

REUNITED: A MIRACLE MARRIAGE

BY
JUDY CAMPBELL

MILLS
BOON®
™

First published in Great Britain 2011
by Mills & Boon,
an imprint of Harlequin (UK) Limited,
Large Print edition 2011
Eton House, 18-24 Paradise Road,
Richmond, Surrey TW9 1SR

© Judy Campbell 2011

ISBN: 978 0 263 21759 9

Harlequin (UK) policy is to use papers that are
natural, renewable and recyclable products and made
from wood grown in sustainable forests. The logging
and manufacturing process conform to the legal
environmental regulations of the country of origin.

Printed and bound in Great Britain
by CPI Antony Rowe, Chippenham, Wiltshire

Judy Campbell is from Cheshire. As a teenager she spent a great year at high school in Oregon, USA, as an exchange student. She has worked in a variety of jobs, including teaching young children, being a secretary and running a small family business. Her husband comes from a medical family, and one of their three grown-up children is a GP. Any spare time—when she's not writing romantic fiction—is spent playing golf, especially in the Highlands of Scotland.

Recent titles by the same author:

FROM SINGLE MUM TO LADY
GP'S MARRIAGE WISH

To the happy memory of my mother

CHAPTER ONE

IT WAS stuffy in the lecture theatre, and the professor of cardiac medicine had a monotonous, droning voice. Sally Lawson smothered a yawn and looked around the room, amused to see that a few people had given up the unequal fight and were quietly nodding off to sleep. She knew exactly how they felt.

Her gaze wandered over the audience, wondering if she recognised any of the people there besides Jean Cornwell, her colleague, who was sitting next to her.

Suddenly she blinked, jerked out of her lethargy as she noticed a man several rows below her, or rather the back of a man's head. Of course it wasn't…it couldn't possibly be him, could it? She shifted in her seat to try and see the man from a different angle as from where she was sitting he looked amazingly like Jack

McLennan. A funny little tremor of apprehension fluttered through her even thinking of his name. Odd how just seeing the back of a stranger who had the same thick russet hair and broad shoulders of a man she used to love long ago could kick-start all kinds of memories…

Sally leaned forward to get a closer look at this guy's profile. Of course Jack McLennan was hundreds of miles away in Australia and had been for years—he was probably director of the Australian health service by now, or something equally imposing, she thought wryly. She gazed into space, the professor's lecture a mere background drone to her thoughts. It had been six years since she'd last seen Jack, the love of her life—six years since he'd told her out of the blue that he wanted to finish their affair and concentrate on his career. And she'd thought she'd known the man so well after their year's passionate affair—they had even discussed marriage. She would never have guessed that he had been using her, had just wanted a fling before he finished his training and disappeared….at least, that was how it had seemed to her.

The lecture was drawing to a close, and the professor's voice rose slightly, bringing Sally back to the present.

'And so, ladies and gentlemen, I hope I've given you some insight into the challenges of treating hypertension and the benefits of tackling a major cause of cardiovascular disease as early and aggressively as possible.'

He beamed around the hall and there was enthusiastic applause from the audience, glad of the chance to stretch their legs at last. People began to get up from their seats and hurry away from the hall, amongst them the man who'd caught Sally's eye. It was extraordinary—even the way he held his head slightly to one side as he listened to the person talking to him was so like one of Jack's mannerisms. He was laughing, his deep-toned voice carrying over the crowd, and it could have been Jack's voice—that easy laugh reminding her that, despite everything that had happened, they'd had a lot of fun together.

Sally picked up her handbag and started to follow Jean out of the lecture hall. Of course, it was neither here nor there that a strange man at the other side of the room should remind her of Jack and their long-ago affair. After all, she was engaged now and going to be married very soon.

'What time do you want to be off tomorrow, Sally?' Jean asked. Sally was contemplating the figure now moving towards the exit of the hall.

Jean waited a few seconds for a response then, grinning, dug her friend gently in the ribs. 'Hey! You're in another universe, aren't you?'

'What? Oh…yes, sorry. I thought I saw someone I used to work with, but it can't be him—I believe he works abroad now. What did you say?'

'Tomorrow—when do you want to leave? There's a lecture in the morning but do you mind if we go after breakfast? If you want to stay, I can always get a lift back to Crachan from someone else.'

'Suits me to leave early,' said Sally absently, her eyes drifting back to that tall figure. 'I think

I know all I want to know about cardiac health at the moment, thank you!'

Suddenly the man turned round and Sally gave a quick shocked intake of breath, her whole body stiffening in amazement. Good God! She wasn't imagining a likeness, no doubt about it—it really was Jack! She looked in stupefaction at the good-looking, strong face and the lock of hair falling over his forehead as it always used to…and the years fell away as she saw the man who'd given her the most gloriously romantic time of her life—and had then broken her heart so cruelly and inexplicably six years ago.

For a second his eyes locked with hers before he turned away, and then suddenly he did a double-take, a frown of uncertainty flickering across his face as he stared at her in puzzlement. Then his eyes widened in recognition and, mumbling something to the person beside him, he began to make his way through the crowd towards her.

Sally stood rooted to the spot, gazing at him in disbelief until he was standing before her and those familiar periwinkle-blue eyes set in a tanned open face held hers in total amazement. The babble in the hall seemed to recede and for a few moments it was as if there were just the two of them alone together.

'Oh, my God—it's Sally, Sally Lawson,' he said softly.

He had a lovely voice, deep and warm, and it brought all sorts of memories tumbling back through Sally's mind—quite unsuitable memories considering she was engaged to another man now. The first time Jack had kissed her, the feel of his body against hers when they'd danced, the first time they'd… She swallowed hard. She was damned if she was going to go overboard welcoming Dr Jack McLennan. Since he'd left her after a year together, there'd never been a letter or a phone call to ask how she was—not even a Christmas card. He'd treated her abominably and she couldn't forget that.

She pulled herself together and stood tall, gazing at him steadily. 'Why, hello,' she said coolly. 'I…I didn't expect to see you here. I thought you lived in Australia now.'

His eyes hadn't left her face, raking her

features as if to convince himself that it was her. 'Sally Lawson!' he repeated, ignoring her remark about Australia. 'What a surprise!' His lips curved in that slightly lopsided smile of his that used to melt her heart. 'At least, that's what you were called six years ago. I guess your name could be something else now.'

Sally swallowed hard, a lot of confused emotions flooding through her. Jack still had that rangy, athletic figure that looked as if he ran ten miles a day, and the power to send any girl's pulse racing—his physical presence was as potent as it ever had been. But damn him—the man had broken her heart once and led her up the garden path. He was a deceiving rat! She forced a stiff smile.

'Yes,' she admitted. 'I'm still Sally Lawson—for the moment. How are you, Jack?'

'Just fine. It's good to see you again. I wasn't quite sure it was you for a moment because your hair's different.' He paused for a second, his glance sweeping over her. 'It suits you short like that.'

Could Sally see any change in him? Not really.

He'd kept time at bay very well—a hint of grey around the temples, a few more lines creasing the corners of his eyes perhaps. She saw his glance flicker over her hands, obviously noting her engagement ring with its enormous glinting diamond. Tim liked flamboyant gestures and wouldn't have entertained buying his fiancée something restrained. She put her other hand over it almost protectively. Funny how heavy it felt and how huge it looked on her slim finger— almost as if it were shouting, Look at me! I'm getting married to someone who's loaded! She had to admit that sometimes she felt it was a tad ostentatious.

'I see you're engaged,' he remarked lightly.

She nodded. 'Yes…I'm getting married in a few weeks.' She was about to ask him if he was married and then thought better of it. She wasn't interested in his domestic life, was she? It was better to stick to work-related matters.

She said flippantly, 'And what brings you to Glasgow? I'd have thought you were running the Australian health service by now. Did you reach the top of the ladder?'

'What?' He suddenly looked discomfited, as if reminded of the career he'd told her he'd wanted to follow rather than carry on with their relationship. Then he said briefly, 'It worked out fine—but my mother died suddenly, and I came back for her funeral. I've a younger brother just starting at university so I decided to stay to keep my eye on him.'

Sally flicked a look at his bleak expression. 'Oh, that's sad…about your mother I mean. It must have been hard for you.'

She felt a flash of sympathy for him. Obviously his mother had died before he'd been able to see her again. In the year she'd gone out with Jack she had never met his parents—they had lived in a village in the wilds of the Highlands. There was a short silence and the sound of the voices in the room reasserted themselves. Sally suddenly realised that Jean was waiting patiently by her side.

'Oh, sorry, Jean. This is Jack McLennan, an old…er…colleague of mine from my days at St. Mary's hospital six years ago. We did our A and E rotation together. Jack, this is Jean

Cornwell, the senior partner in the G.P. practice I work for.'

Jack took his gaze off Sally and turned to shake Jean's hand. 'So are you local?' he asked.

'We're on the west coast in a town called Crachan. Sally and I thought we'd take up the offer of two nights in Glasgow being pampered at a good hotel with this refresher course in cardiac care,' explained Jean.

Jack grinned. 'That echoes my thoughts too. I'm doing a locum job in a practice round here but it comes to an end soon, so I'll be looking for somewhere else for a few months before I start a permanent job in the autumn.'

Jean turned to Sally with a broad smile. 'Aha! Hear that Sal? Someone who wants a temporary job! That could be helpful!'

Sally felt her stomach give a nervous little jump of anticipation at what she was sure Jean was going to say next. 'Oh, I don't think Jack would be interested in our practice,' she intercepted quickly.

'Why on earth not?' asked Jean, arching an eyebrow. 'Surely it's not as bad as all that!'

'Well, it's a bit of a backwater...'

Sally bit her lip. It shouldn't matter to her whether Jack McLennan worked at the practice or not—as long as he was good at his job, that was the important thing wasn't it? After all, he meant nothing whatsoever to her now. Perhaps a lingering sadness that she'd misread his character and not realised that he was an opportunistic creep underneath that charismatic veneer, regret over the wasted years of sadness after their break-up—but maybe the real reason was that she didn't feel like revisiting the past if they became colleagues again.

Jack looked from one woman to the other. 'What's this about, then? Are you looking for someone to work with you?'

Jean nodded. 'I want to go and help out my sister in New Zealand—she's in her third pregnancy and her husband is in hospital himself after a bad car crash. I'd like to go over for three months, so Sally's going to need help in the practice. She just mentioned that she used to work with you at St. Mary's so at least you'd know each other.'

He flicked a glance at Sally as if aware of her misgivings, his blue eyes slighted hooded. 'Perhaps you'd better discuss it with each other...'

'A good idea,' cut in Sally hastily. 'There are one or two local people who might do locum work with us.'

'That's true.' Jean nodded. 'Although it's mostly a week here or there, nothing very sustained. It would be good to get someone who could do the whole three months and get to know the patients. Anyway, if you'd like to come and discuss it with us, this is our number.' Jean gave him a card and smiled at Sally. 'Come on—let's get some lunch and maybe go for a shop this afternoon to wake us up after that fascinating lecture.'

'A good idea,' agreed Sally. She looked coolly at Jack. 'Goodbye,' she said in an offhand voice.

They walked out of the lecture hall and Jack McLennan stared after them. He might have gone anywhere this weekend—to stay in London with friends, go walking in the hills—but he had to choose at the last minute to come

to this particular conference. He felt as if someone had hit him hard in the solar plexus, He
hadn't realised how devastating it would be to
see Sally Lawson again. She was still a knock-
out, with those smoky grey eyes and honey-
blonde hair cut now in a thick bob that framed
her face—and still with the power to knock him
sideways. He clenched his fists in his trouser
pockets, trying to get to grips with the fact that
he'd just come face to face with the girl he could
have married six years ago—the girl he should
have married if circumstances had been different.

He started to walk slowly out of the hall,
heedless of the crowds milling around him,
and allowed himself to step back in time as the
emotions he'd felt then came back with vivid
intensity. He had realised that he had to finish
their romance and by a twist of circumstance it
had happened at the end of the hospital annual
ball. Sally had looked absolutely stunning in a
sheath silk dress of ice blue, showing off her
curvaceous figure beautifully, and there had
been a particular bitter-sweet intensity about

their happiness for him, knowing that by the end of the evening he would leave her for ever. Like the rewinding of a film, he could still visualise so clearly her bewildered face as he'd told her that he needed to get away to fulfil his medical ambitions.

At first she'd laughed. 'You, Jack McLennan? Concentrate on your career? You've got to be joking!' She'd looked up at him impishly. 'You're too fond of your sport and…other things,' she'd said coquettishly, putting her arms around him. 'You're not getting rid of me that easily!'

He hadn't reacted, just looked back at her rather grimly, trying to keep his emotions under control, and her eyes had widened in disbelief as eventually she'd realised that he'd meant what he'd said. Tears had slowly rolled down her cheeks, and it had been unbearable for him to witness her distress. He'd been deliberately brutal because Sally had needed to be under no illusion that things could ever be rekindled between them—he hadn't been able to tell her what had lain behind his decision.

Oh, yes, his career had flourished in Australia.

He'd worked hard, plunged himself into his job heart and soul, trying to put Sally and the nightmare scenario of what had happened in his family out of his mind, and the terror that he might end up like his father—a drunken brute who'd terrorised those around him.

He flicked a glance at his watch and sighed as he went to pick up his key at Reception. He'd have to go to the dinner tonight—there were several old friends at the conference he'd promised to catch up with, but he'd check out of the hotel first thing the next day, and out of Sally Lawson's life once more. He had no rights over her—she was some other lucky beggar's girlfriend, and looking at her expression when they'd been standing face to face a few minutes before had told him very plainly that the only emotion she felt towards him was dislike.

'So, Sally, tell me about this Jack McLennan you used to work with.' In the steamy atmosphere of the little café, Jean looked at Sally enquiringly. 'I got the impression you were less than enthusiastic when I suggested he apply for the job. Didn't you get on, or was he no good?'

Sally shrugged. 'Oh, he was a good doctor, no doubt about that—very committed.' She chose her words carefully, unwilling to reveal by any inflection in her voice that he'd meant anything to her at all. 'He was very ambitious, actually—I'm sure he had a terrific job.'

'But what about working with him again?' persisted Jean. 'Any objections?'

Sally stirred her coffee slowly and stared at the swirling liquid. 'We...well, I suppose you could say we had a difference of opinion just before he left.'

'A pity,' observed Jean, 'But perhaps you could learn to overlook your differences now. After all, it's a few years ago since you worked together. I must say he looked rather pleasant.' She laughed. 'Actually, he looks absolutely gorgeous! I'm surprised you didn't fall for him, Sal.'

'Oh, everyone fell for Jack McLennan,' said Sally offhandedly. She put her cup down on the table rather abruptly and stood up and stretched.

'Now we've had lunch, I think I'll go and have a run in the park before we meet this evening, Jean, if you don't mind—need to get rid of a few cobwebs. See you later.'

Jean looked thoughtfully after Sally as she left the restaurant, then shrugged her shoulders as her mobile started ringing. Sally didn't notice Jean answer her mobile phone, or see her expression as she answered it.

Sally unlocked the door of her room and went straight to the bathroom, peeling off her tracksuit as she went. After an hour's run on a sunny afternoon, she was hot and dripping, but she felt invigorated and more positive—all that exercise after the unsettling meeting with Jack had helped to calm her down. It had been a shock—no, she corrected herself quickly, more a surprise, meeting him again, but her life had moved on and now she was embroiled in the excitement of getting everything ready for her wedding. It was going to be fun, albeit her instinct had been to go for a low-key ceremony, but Tim was very keen to invite everyone he knew, including business acquaintances, 'because it will help enormously in getting my name known in the right circles, Sally,' he'd explained.

She turned on the shower and stood under the hot water gratefully, turning her body so that the little sharp needles of spray reached all over her, and then she stepped out, her skin tingling. She grabbed a towel, wound it round her wet hair and put on the towelling robe hanging up in the bathroom. She would make herself a cup of tea and watch the news on television before getting ready for the evening's dinner, then probably ring Tim and tell him she'd be home by lunchtime the next day.

Just as she was picking up her mobile to make the call, a peremptory knock on the door made her jump—it was probably room service, she decided, although she hadn't ordered anything.

'Yes?' she called out. 'Who is it?'

A short silence and then a deep voice replied, 'It's Jack—Jack McLennan. I've got a message for you.'

Jack McLennan? What on earth was he doing

here? Six years with no contact, and suddenly he thinks it's OK to buttonhole her in her hotel bedroom! Sally drew the bathrobe round her body tightly and walked to the door, glancing at her flustered image in the mirror as she passed. A feeling of unease flickered through her. She didn't want to see Jack again—she simply had no interest in the man, and she resented the fact that for some reason his appearance had disturbed her.

She certainly didn't want to see him when she was dressed in a skimpy bathrobe with a towel over her hair…once upon a time it might have been only too wonderful to be dressed in next to nothing with Jack McLennan in a hotel bedroom, but not now, not now…Coming to see her just had to be curiosity on his part, an excuse to see her again so that they could have a cosy chat about past times…and that was the last thing she was going to do with a man who'd treated her so badly.

She didn't open the door, but called out crisply, 'Who's the message from?'

'Your colleague, Jean Cornwell.'

'Jean? Why should she give you a message—why not give it me herself?'

'She's had bad news and hadn't time to get it to you. If you open the door, I can give you her note.'

Anxiety fluttered through Sally and she opened the door. 'OK. Pass it to me.'

A pair of deep blue eyes held hers for a moment then swept quickly over her attire.

'Sorry—rather an inconvenient time I guess,' he apologised.

Sally pulled the robe even more tightly round herself, acutely aware of how close they were to each other. The last time they'd been this close, she thought fleetingly, had been when Jack had been finishing with her and he'd looked so stern…so implacable. Was he reminded of that time, or had it meant so little to him that he'd forgotten that episode completely? He'd probably had many affairs since then and their liaison had been long forgotten. She took the note from him, pushing those silly thoughts to the back of her mind.

'Do you know what this is all about?' she asked curtly, tearing open the envelope.

'Yes—Jean bumped into me in the foyer in a very distressed state. Apparently she'd just had a phone call to say that her sister in New Zealand has been admitted to hospital with pre-eclampsia, and with her husband still in hospital himself the situation is very difficult. She tried to ring you on her mobile, but couldn't get a signal.'

Sally looked at him in distress. 'Oh, no! Poor Jean! She must be worried sick. What's she going to do?'

'She's gone to Glasgow to get a flight, I think, but the thing is, Sally, she was extremely concerned that you would be on your own and begged me to take on the locum job at your practice. Anyway, I guess it's all in the note.'

Sally frowned. 'As we said before, there are other people who can help out—I can ring them when I get back to Crachan. There's no need for you to…trouble yourself.'

'Apparently she did ring your contacts but none of them can start immediately. However, it's up to you, Sally. Do you think we could work together…again?'

'Possibly,' she replied coldly, suddenly angry that he should imagine she would be in any way affected by what had happened years ago. She had a fiancé, she was getting married soon. It didn't matter to her who she worked with as long as they were competent.

Her eyes scanned Jean's note quickly. Jean was obviously in a state, worrying about her sister's family and indeed her sister's health.

'So sorry to land you in it like this,' Sally read. 'Gail is very ill, and although neighbours are looking after her children for the time being, I feel I must get over there as soon as possible. I'm going to try and catch a flight from Glasgow to Heathrow tonight and get to New Zealand from there. Do you think you could possibly work with Jack McLennan for a few weeks? After all, he's available immediately, unlike everyone else, and he seems to have lots of experience. He was rather reluctant to take on the job without your sanction, but it really would rest my mind if I thought there was someone to help you out—and we don't seem to have many takers. Text me when you can. Love, Jean.'

Sally stuffed the note in her pocket. There didn't seem to be much choice in the matter—it was true she needed help and she knew Jack was a good doctor.

Jack watched her reaction. 'I wouldn't want to put you in an awkward position if you have any reservations about working with me,' he said gently.

'Why should I?' remarked Sally rather tersely. 'It was a long time ago when we went our separate ways, and a lot's happened since then.'

'That's true.' He nodded. 'You've got engaged, for one thing. When are you getting married?'

'In two months—that's one of the reasons we need a locum who will know the practice quite well, because I'll be going on my honeymoon for a week after the wedding.'

Jack's brows lifted slightly. 'Only a week?' he remarked teasingly, 'Why doesn't he grab the chance for longer than that?'

'Tim's got a very busy schedule with his business at the moment.'

'Ah, I see. He's a businessman, then?'

'Yes—he can't be away from work for too long,' replied Sally rather defensively. The thought flickered through her head that Tim might be just as career-orientated as Jack was—but he did at least want to commit to her! 'Anyway,' she added briskly, 'about you joining the practice…'

She paused for a second as a feeling of anxiety flickered through her. Could she really work with this man who had once meant so much to her? She took a deep breath. She was engaged and what had happened between her and Jack was completely irrelevant now. The fact was that in weeks of advertising for a locum to help at the surgery, no one suitable had come forward so she had to be sensible.

'I guess we can stand each other for a month or two until Jean gets back,' she said.

'I guess we can,' he commented lightly. 'When do you want me to start?'

'Come in two days and I'll have sorted out your accommodation…' She paused for a second. 'You didn't tell me if you have a family.

The flat I'm thinking of isn't suitable for children.'

He smiled faintly. 'No...no children or wives accumulated over six years—just a teenage brother at university in Glasgow.'

He was probably still too focussed on his damn career, Sally reflected scornfully. A man who refused to be tied down in a relationship. But an odd feeling of satisfaction flickered through her at this information.

'Well,' she said briskly, 'you've got our card with the address on—it should take you about an hour to get there.'

'I'll look forward to it,' he murmured, and walked off down the corridor.

He smiled grimly to himself. He was under no illusions about Sally's feelings towards him. She didn't like him, but she was in a tight spot and needed help—and though his first instinct had been to get out of her life again now she was engaged, somehow the opportunity to work with the woman he knew he'd never really stopped loving was irresistible. Not, he thought sadly, that the situation had changed. He still couldn't offer her a future. And as usual when he thought about the reason he was still single, he felt a tremor of horror, which, even after six years, hadn't diminished.

Sally went back into the room, peeled off the towel round her head and sat down in front of the dressing table. She stared at herself in the mirror and a pale, worried face stared back at her. It must be because she was tired that her heart was banging against her rib cage like a drum and her mouth was so dry. She should be mightily relieved that someone she knew who was good at their job was going to fill in at the practice. It was just that working with someone she'd once been so close to would be rather… strange, but she would keep her distance and soon get used to it. Then she picked up the hair-dryer and began to dry her hair.

CHAPTER TWO

SALLY stood by the window of her surgery, looking out over the sea to the little isle of Hersa. Her mood was as restless as the white-capped waves lashing against the sea-wall as she waited for the arrival of Jack McLennan. How stupid it was to be so nervous about working with him, she thought irritably. After all, he would merely be a colleague, someone she could keep at a distance. She felt quite neutral about him—of course she did, she told herself sharply. Some old feelings might have been stirred up momentarily when she'd seen him again, but the aching sadness mixed with hatred she'd felt for him when he'd dumped her so shockingly six years ago had diminished now. All the same, she had to get used to the idea of working with someone who had once betrayed her.

Over time, she'd learned to live without Jack,

although it had been a slow and painful process. She'd felt rootless and alone. There'd been liaisons with a few men, none of them permanent, none of them able to offer her the settled life she craved. She seemed to live in a world of happy couples, many of whom were starting families. Gradually, however, she'd reconciled herself to the life of a singleton, and had thrown herself into taking up as many interests as she could.

Then, only a few months ago, she'd met Tim Langley, a man going places big time with an IT company in Glasgow, having built it up from nothing. He had sown his wild oats and was longing to get married, and Sally was everything he'd pictured a wife of his should be—successful in her own right, beautiful, and connected to the right people.

She had met Tim through her father, whose well-known firm of solicitors acted for Tim's company. Mr Lawson was a respected lawyer in Glasgow, very much involved in the city life, and he admired Tim's get-up-and-go and ambition and had encouraged his daughter and Tim to get together. Her parents had been devastated at their daughter's unhappiness when she and Jack had broken up and had longed for her to find stability and love again. They had been thrilled when her new romance had seemed to be going well.

At first she and Tim had been thrown together when asked to make up numbers for business parties that Mr Lawson had arranged. They'd become good friends and it had been fun to be part of a group. They suited each other and it seemed right that two lonely people should end up together. Perhaps they were both aware that their commitment to each other was based more on need for a partner than all-consuming passion, but once they'd decided to get married, and almost before she'd known it, Sally had been caught up in the whirlwind of organising the wedding.

In two weeks she was having the final fitting of her wedding dress, although she felt a little shiver of guilt at the expense of it. But Tim had said that she must have only the best—and that was rather flattering. Sally had to dress for the part even if she did sometimes feel that she was being asked to take the lead in an enormous dramatic production on behalf of the guests.

She let the window blind drop with a snap and turned back towards her desk with a small sigh, flicking a look at her watch. It was still early—half an hour before surgery began—so she'd just have time to do some paperwork and catch up on her hospital admission e-mails.

Joyce Farquahar's abrupt voice came over the intercom. 'Dr McLennan's here to see you. Do you want me to send him in?'

An inexplicable skip of her heart at this information made Sally tell herself sternly, *For heaven's sake, you're only working with Jack because it's an emergency situation. Forget what went on between you all that time ago. He's a colleague, that's all!*

Then she said aloud, 'Thanks, Joyce. And if you'd rustle up some coffee, that would be great.'

Joyce said in her usual brusque manner, 'I can't do everything at once. It'll be a few minutes if you want me to finish printing off all the immunisation letters first.'

Sally grinned to herself. Joyce Farquahar was hard working and well organised, but charm didn't feature in her many attributes. 'I think the letters can wait a few minutes,' she said drily.

A few seconds later there was a light knock on the door and Jack walked in, looking tall and imposing in a well-cut dark suit that emphasised his strong build. There were no two ways about it, he had style! How well she remembered those compelling blue eyes with the dancing amusement in them that had made her go weak at the knees. Sally drew in a deep breath. It was hard to believe that underneath that debonair and charismatic aura he was a complete rat! She wondered how many other women he'd conned over the years.

He smiled down at her easily, and before she knew it had taken her hand in his in a firm handshake. 'I'm looking forward to working with you again, Sally,' he said in that deep attractive voice.

His hand was warm and strong and Sally removed hers quickly from his clasp. 'We won't be working in each other's pockets,' she informed him coolly. 'Once I've shown you the ropes we'll have a weekly meeting. Jean and I divided up the clinics between us and I guess we can do the same.'

'Whatever you say.'

A wry look of amusement flickered in Jack's eyes. He didn't blame her for keeping him at arm's length. From her point of view he was the man whose word couldn't be trusted, the man who had led her to believe they'd had a future together, and she was bound to hate him for what he'd done to her. He'd thought it would be for the best for her to think of him as a heartless brute, someone not worth loving, and that way she'd get over him quickly, realising that she'd made a mistake and get on with her life.

Over the years he'd often wondered what she was doing, what path her life had taken. Seeing her standing in front of him now dressed in a trim navy blue trousersuit, with those wide grey eyes and blond, shining hair, he realised that his feelings for her were still very near the surface. Only now it was too late, he thought sadly. Even if he had been able to commit to her, she was about to get married to somebody else.

She cleared her throat and said briskly, 'Then shall we get on with things? Please sit down and I'll give you the lowdown on the practice before we start work, and later I'll show you the little flat above the surgery where you can stay—we've just had it renovated.'

If Jack noticed her peremptory manner he didn't show it. 'Sounds a good idea,' he said evenly, hitching up his trousers and sitting down on the chair in front of the desk. 'It'll be very convenient to live over the shop. Do you live near the practice?'

'I have a little cottage at the end of the village.'

Jack's gaze slid to the picture of Tim on her desk and turned it more towards him. 'And is this your fiancé?'

'Yes… He lives in Glasgow,' she replied, slightly irritated at his probing questions. She continued crisply, 'He comes here at the weekends when he can—or I go to stay with him.' She turned the conversation firmly back to the matter in hand. 'Now, about the practice—we have six thousand patients scattered over a wide area, and I'm afraid we're responsible for an on-call service at night, which we share with two other practices down the coast, but we only do it once a week. I hope that won't be a problem?'

Jack shook his head and looked out of the window where the view could just be seen through the half-closed blinds. 'It's a lovely area to work in,' he commented. 'Do we have any patients on the island over there?'

Sally nodded. 'Yes—there's a ferry that comes and goes, but the sea can be treacherous. Although the island is so near it means that the ferry can't always get across and in an emergency the rescue helicopter has to be used.'

There was a loud bang on the door and Joyce stumped in with a tray of coffee. 'Here you are, then. I'm afraid there's no sugar left,' she said tersely, putting the tray on the desk. 'I'll send Sharon out for some when she gets here.'

Sharon was the other receptionist, a constant thorn in Joyce's side, giggly and good-natured and addicted to women's magazines with the latest tips on how to improve oneself—which she was always trying to persuade Joyce to follow, without much success.

'Joyce, this is Jack McLennan, who's going to be helping out while Jean's in New Zealand.'

Jack stood up and smiled down at Joyce. 'A pleasure to meet you. I'll be relying on you to keep me on the straight and narrow!'

He gave her that melting lopsided grin, and even as Sally watched, Jean's dour face relaxed into an unwilling smile.

'Och, I'll be pleased to help if I can. Just let me know if you're not sure about anything,' she said as she went out.

Jack obviously hadn't lost his skill in turning on the charm, thought Sally, almost amused by his ability to bring a smile to Joyce's face. Thank goodness she herself was immune to it now! She opened one of the desk drawers to give Jack a sheaf of papers relating to the practice and the local health authority, and just as she did so, loud screaming started outside.

They both looked up, startled, then Jack

frowned and put down his coffee, getting up from his chair and striding to the window.

'Sounds as if someone's in trouble,' he murmured, pulling aside the blinds to look outside. He gave a sudden horrified exclamation as he leaned forward to look at the scene.

'My God!' he exclaimed. 'There's someone in the water, and it's hellish rough. A little girl's watching it from the side—she's the one that's screaming. I'd better go and see if I can do anything.' He dashed out of the room and Sally gazed openmouthed after him, before pulling herself together and running after him through the waiting room.

'Get the emergency services, Joyce. It looks like someone needs rescuing from the sea,' she shouted as she followed him.

Outside she stood transfixed. A few yards out, a man and a dog were being tossed like corks on the surface of the heaving sea. Waves were crashing against the breakwater, throwing white spume into the air. Clinging to the railings overlooking the sea a small child was screaming, and Jack was pulling off his clothes frantically, preparing to dive into the water. Sally ran up to the child and put her arms round her.

'It's all right, sweetheart, don't worry. Help's on its way very soon. You come inside with me for a minute…'

The child clung obstinately to the railings. 'I want my grandpa and Fudge,' she screamed. 'Get them out.'

Sally had to get the little girl away from watching this scenario. A traumatic scene like this could stay with the child for the rest of her life and she didn't want her to witness a tragedy if they couldn't get the man out of the water soon. She bent down, picked up the struggling child and took her into the surgery.

'Joyce!' she shouted above the child's crying, 'Can you get this little one a drink and a biscuit and distract her while I go back and see if there are any lifebelts?'

Joyce might normally have an abrupt manner, but in an emergency she was a stalwart. She took the little girl behind the desk, talking soothingly to her all the time, then sat her on her knee with some milk and began showing her a comic from the waiting room. Sally dashed out again and ran to the lifebelt fixture on the wall a short distance away.

'My God,' she muttered. 'The damn thing's been vandalised!'

She stared at the rusting remnants of the hooks that had held the lifebelt in place—obviously it had been stolen. She looked back at Jack, now stripped down to his underpants, his suit and shirt flung in a heap on the ground behind him, preparing to leap into the water. It was still early in the day and the road as yet was deserted. There was no one to help.

'Wait, Jack!' she screamed. 'Let me get a rope from somewhere…please!'

'No time!' he shouted back. 'Don't worry!'

Sally caught her breath as he dropped into the water and began to swim laboriously towards the bobbing heads of the man and dog, making slow headway in the heaving water. She looked around desperately—what the hell could she use to help him? His head kept disappearing in the swell of the waves. Each time she thought he'd gone, and then he'd reappear again slightly nearer the stricken man. Where was everybody? To her immense relief, a van came down the road, and Sally ran up to it, waving for it to stop. It drew into the kerb and a burly man dressed in overalls got out.

'What's the matter?' he asked.

She pointed breathlessly to the sea and the man and dog in the water. 'Have you got a rope…anything to throw to them?' she yelled.

Without a word the man opened the doors and miraculously produced a coil of thick nylon rope.

'I'll get it to them—don't you worry,' he shouted.

Sally watched on tenterhooks as he quickly tied one end of the rope to the railings, then he took off his overalls and within a few moments had also jumped into the water, holding the rope as he did so. People were beginning to gather round now and all of them watched tensely, murmuring to each other as the two men tried to reach the man struggling tantalisingly close to them but behind a great wall of waves.

Jack was a strong swimmer, that was easy

to tell, but even so it took him a nerve-racking few minutes to get within touching distance of the distressed man. The man was panicking, shouting and throwing his arms up, and when Jack took hold of him he struggled, clutching at Jack's neck so that it was impossible to get a firm hold of the man to tow him back.

Sally gripped the railing, her eyes glued to the drama being played out before her, willing Jack to calm the man so that he could be helped. Gradually the van driver, although not as good a swimmer as Jack, made headway towards them and somehow they both managed, despite the heavy swell, to pass the rope round the man's chest.

At least now there was a lifeline to be used, and people rushed to hold the rope and started pulling it towards the wall. The man was shouting something—difficult over the roar of the waves to hear what it was but suddenly Jack veered away from escorting him back and made for the bobbing head of the dog. There was a groan of dismay from the crowd.

'Don't do that!' shouted Sally desperately. 'You'll drown! Oh, you stupid, stupid man!'

He didn't hear her, of course, and continued doggedly making his way towards the animal. By a miraculous sudden stroke of luck the swell pushed the dog towards him. He grabbed its collar and slowly, very slowly, managed to gain ground towards the shore. Sally started to make her way carefully down the slippery steps, ignoring people's cries to keep back. She bent down to grab the animal as Jack, the van driver and the rescued man were hauled up by one or two of the onlookers. She kept hold of the dog with grim determination, soaked by the spray from breaking waves against the wall, and then she too was helped back up the steps.

An overwhelming sense of relief flooded through her—they were all safe! Jack was standing feet away from her, bent over double, his hands on his knees, chest heaving as he caught his breath. Then he was handed a towel and started briskly towelling himself dry. There was no disguising his impressive physique: he was still as tautly muscled as he'd been when he and Sally had been together. He stood up and looked across at her, feeling her gaze at him, and Sally turned away abruptly. What a stupid observation to make, she told herself crossly. There was an emergency to be dealt with!

She squatted down by the rescued man, now laid out on the ground on someone's coat, and recognised him immediately as a patient at the Harbour Practice—a man of over seventy. She put her fingers on his wrist, checking his pulse, noting his shallow breathing and that his lips were tinged blue. His eyes tried to focus on her, but he seemed confused and rather drowsy.

'Callum,' she said loudly, trying to rouse him. 'We're going to try and warm you up a bit before the ambulance gets here.' She turned round and saw Sharon hovering anxiously nearby.

'Get plenty of blankets from the surgery, Sharon, and bring a few mugs of warm coffee— not too hot.'

Sharon tottered off in the high heels she always wore to work, then in the distance Sally heard the whine of an ambulance siren. She took hold of the man's hand and squeezed it. 'You'll be all right—the paramedics are here.'

The man mumbled something and she bent down to hear him. 'The dog. What happened to the dog…and my little granddaughter?'

'The dog's going to be fine. Don't worry, he's wrapped in a blanket and I can see him wagging his tail now! And as for your granddaughter, she's in the surgery across the road, being well looked after.'

This was no time to tell Callum how foolish he'd been in trying to rescue the dog by himself—and she reflected grimly that two other people could have drowned trying to rescue the man in trouble.

A few minutes later the ambulance drew up in front of them and a paramedic leapt out, quickly assessing the scene before him. He recognised Sally and came up to her, squatting down next to Callum and feeling the man's pulse.

'Hello, Dr Lawson.' His eyes swept round the group of people. 'Looks like a few of you are rather damp. I take it this gentleman's been in that cold water for a while—do you know his name?'

'Yes, it's Callum Brody, he's a patient of ours and he's about seventy-three years old. His pulse is slow, about sixty-five per minute, and as you can see he's cyanosed and drowsy.'

'Definitely hypothermic,' agreed the paramedic. He slipped his hand into the man's armpit. 'This is an area of his body that should be warm, but it feels quite cold.'

He turned to his colleague who was standing nearby, watching them. 'Get some space blankets out of the van—enough for this patient and the two men over there,' he said, indicating Jack and the van driver. He looked at Sally. 'Looks like you could do with a blanket too—you're shivering. We'll get you one, and then you go straight inside.'

Sally didn't object when she was wrapped in a space blanket with its layers of heat-reflecting material. She felt exhausted and her whole body shivered. Jack came up to her, also enveloped in a blanket.

'That was a narrow squeak,' he remarked.

Relief at their safety made her sound waspish. 'You shouldn't have gone in until we'd got you a rope,' she said brusquely to Jack. 'And you're to go in the ambulance to be checked out at the Rannoch Hospital.'

Jack laughed. 'Certainly not! I'm a bit chilled, but I'll get warm in the surgery and my clothes are dry.'

'But you ought to—'

'No "ought to" about it. I've come to start work today, and that's what I'm going to do.'

The paramedics had loaded Callum Brody into the ambulance and came forward to try and persuade Jack and Des, the van driver, to come with them to be checked over, but they both refused, Des saying he preferred to go home and get warm. Sally was left alone with Jack.

'You should have gone for a check-up—you were in the water for ages,' she said brusquely.

'You're a doctor—you can check me over,' he replied cheekily with a grin.

She couldn't help smiling back at him and briefly there was a tremor between them of… what? A slight rapport, a ripple of the old attraction? Perhaps it was just relief. The incident had had a happy conclusion—without Jack's quick intervention Callum and the dog would probably have drowned. It had been foolhardy of Jack, but courageous to say the least. He hadn't stopped to think of his own safety, she had to acknowledge that.

'You…you were very impetuous, but very brave,' she murmured. 'You must be freezing.'

He turned to look at her, eyes steely blue through dripping dark hair. 'You can't be too warm yourself. Look at you—you're shivering despite that heat blanket.' Someone had handed him a towel from the practice and he put it round her head, rubbing her hair to dry it. 'You must get those wet things off. Go inside like the paramedic said,' he remarked.

Of course she should go inside, thought Sally, but for a few seconds she stood absolutely still, bowing her head as Jack's strong hands massaged her head and neck with the towel. God, that felt good. She almost forgot she was out on the pavement on a cold and windy day. It was wonderfully relaxing after the tension of the last quarter of an hour. Her body still shook slightly. Perhaps it was a reactive response to the situation they'd been through; perhaps it was because he'd pulled her against his shoulders, hugging her comfortingly.

For a brief second time went backwards and she was supported against Jack's familiar hard-muscled body once again. A funny mixture of longing mixed with loss went fleetingly through her. This was how it had once been between them—she leaning against his chest, solid and dependable. She bit her lip, reminding herself that he hadn't been dependable at all. He'd told her he loved her, but that had been a lie. She pulled roughly back from him in embarrassment, flicking her damp hair back from her face. Why the hell had she allowed herself to loll against him in that ridiculous manner? she thought angrily. He mustn't get the impression that he still had any place in her heart. That was in the past now, and her life had turned in a different direction with Tim.

Jack put his hands on her shoulders and smiled down at her. 'Go inside and get warm,' he said gently, not giving any sign he was aware of her reaction.

'Of course,' she said lightly. 'We should both go and get ready to start seeing patients.'

They made their way through the small crowd of people that had gathered curiously at the scene of the rescue and went into the surgery. It had begun to fill up, a murmur of conversation floating across to them as patients discussed the recent excitement. Joyce looked up at they went into the office.

'You two ought to get changed,' she said bluntly. 'You'll catch your deaths. By the way, your fiancé's in your room, Sally. I told him you'd been involved in this rescue incident and might be some time but he insisted on waiting. Something to do with his work and the wedding.'

Joyce's tone was slightly caustic. Sally could imagine that she would disapprove of anything she considered 'frivolous' being discussed in surgery hours—one's private life should be kept until after hours was her belief! Briefly Sally also wished that Tim had waited until the evening—at the moment she was cold, wet and tired, with a roomful of patients waiting to be seen. However, that was typical of her fiancé. He was full of pent-up energy, and if he wanted to do something he was impatient to do it immediately. He wasn't the sort of man who could defer anything or wait until a more suitable time—but that was part of his charm, Sally thought fondly: he was always filled with enthusiasm for whatever project he'd got on at the time.

He was on his mobile phone as they came into Sally's room, talking rapidly, but he wheeled round when he heard the door open. 'I'll ring you back—but keep that deal on hold,' he said briskly to the person at the other end of the line, then he snapped the phone shut and put it back in his pocket.

'Ah! Here you are, sweetie!' he exclaimed. 'I've been trying to get hold of you for ages. Finally I got Joyce. She told me there'd been an emergency outside the practice…what happened?'

He leant forward to kiss her then drew back in

a startled fashion, taking in her attire and general dampness. 'Good God, you're all wet, and why are you wearing this blanket? Don't tell me you jumped into the sea as well!' He looked at Jack standing silently by Sally, also muffled in a blanket, and raised his brows. 'Have you both been in the water? What the hell happened?'

Sally laughed. It was typical of her fiancé to turn up unexpectedly and forget that she might be in the middle of work herself!

'It's a long story, Tim, but let me introduce you to Jack McLennan—my new colleague. Jack, this is my fiancé, Tim Langley.'

The two men shook hands and Sally explained rather shakily, 'It's been mayhem here. A man jumped into the water to rescue his dog and got into difficulties. If it hadn't been for Jack leaping in after him, I don't know what would have happened.'

Tim raised his brows, impressed. 'Wow! Did he indeed? Quite a superman! You must be a strong swimmer to help someone in rough seas like this.' He frowned, as if trying to remember something. 'Jack McLennan, eh? Sounds rather familiar. Where have I heard that name before?'

'Jack and I worked together at St. Mary's many years ago…I might have mentioned it,' she said lightly. 'But I thought you were in Glasgow. What are you doing here at this time of the morning?'

'I tried to get here from Glasgow early before you went to work—I wanted to surprise you.' He looked full of suppressed excitement. 'I've been up all night brokering a deal and I think I've managed to swing it. That means mega-bucks in the piggy bank—I couldn't wait to tell you!'

Sally laughed. 'That sounds exciting—we could do with mega-bucks I dare say.'

'I want to tell you all about it of course, but there's another thing that's equally exciting! You won't believe this! I've found a fantastic new venue for our wedding!'

Sally stared at him. 'You've what? But we've already got a lovely place—the Old Hall just by Loch Martin. And we've had all the invitations printed!'

Tim laughed jovially. 'That doesn't matter. It won't take long to get new ones done—and this place is much bigger than the Old Hall. I've thought of several other people it would be politic to invite, especially thinking of your father's position in Glasgow. Fortunately I can get a good deal on it as the premises are owned by a guy I know.'

Sally compressed her lips. Sometimes she felt that Tim was far too impetuous, and although doing things from the best of generous motives, it was slightly unnerving and, she had to admit, rather irritating. Now she suddenly felt unutterably tired and certainly not in the mood to discuss her wedding arrangements in front of Jack.

'I'm sorry, Tim,' she said firmly. 'I need to show Jack the flat above the surgery first of all. He can change there now if he wants. And of course I've got to put on dry clothes— we're both really wet and cold. As you can see, there's a big surgery to get through, and it's Jack's first day here. Why don't we talk about all this tonight?'

Tim pulled a comical face of disappointment. 'Can't you spare ten minutes, Sally? I've been up all night, I'm dead beat, but I've been dying to talk to you about everything.'

Sally bit her lip. Surely Tim could see that it would take her at least a quarter of an hour to change her clothes and she still hadn't put Jack in the picture regarding the computer system. As for Tim being tired, she and Jack were cold and exhausted too! But that was Tim all over, so enthusiastic and buoyed up about everything—he was like a puppy with a new toy.

She tried to mask the impatience in her voice. 'Sorry, Tim, it'll have to wait until later. I'll see you back at the house this evening.'

He shrugged and smiled. 'OK, then—of course I can see you haven't really time for me now. I suppose we'll just have to discuss everything when I see you later.' He turned to Jack and said breezily, 'Well done with the rescue.'

Then a loud jazzy tune from his jacket pocket indicated that his mobile was ringing. He put up a hand of apology and turned away to listen and answer in staccato sentences.

'Ah, Rita! Yes. Fine, I'll be there right away.' He turned back to Sally and Jack. 'Sorry about that! My secretary's very much on the ball and when she says something needs doing, I have to take notice! I must get back to Glasgow pronto, so I'll see you soon—ciao!'

Tim strode out, kissing Sally almost on the run, and Jack watched him through the window as he drove off. He turned round to Sally, one eyebrow raised slightly.

'So that was your fiancé. He sounds a very busy chap. A successful businessman, I guess...'

Sally flicked a look at Jack. His expression was bland, but there was something about his tone... 'What is it?' she asked sharply. 'Don't you like him?'

Jack smiled and shrugged. 'I don't know him at all. He seems...very pleasant. I suppose he's not quite the type of man I would have imagined you marrying.'

Sudden irritation flashed through Sally. How dared Jack, of all people, voice his opinion of Tim?

'Really?' she said sarcastically. 'And what's wrong with him?'

'Nothing that I know of—it's just that you're more a country girl, and he seems very focussed on…well, the world of business, the city.'

Jack didn't actually spell out the words 'You seem ill-matched', but that was what he'd meant, thought Sally furiously. Talk about instant assumptions!

'So he's focussed. I like to see enthusiasm in one's work,' she snapped, putting her hands on her hips and glaring at him. 'Just what are you implying?'

Steady eyes looked at her. 'I'm not implying anything, Sally, but will he settle down in this small community?'

'You don't know him. He's an extremely generous man, quite happy to live in the country when we're married.'

Her cheeks were flushed, large grey eyes sparking with anger, her hair damp and tousled as she raked her hand through it crossly. She looks gorgeous when she's angry, reflected Jack wistfully. It reminded him of times past when they would have a minor tiff and then make it up passionately later. He pushed that thought away savagely—that damn Tim Langley didn't know how lucky he was.

He put up his hands as if in surrender, and said lightly, 'I'm sure he's everything you say he is. You did ask me if I liked him and I'm only voicing my opinion, Sally. No criticism implied, just that he's not what I expected. Perhaps I thought you'd go for someone more—'

'Well, that's neither here nor there, is it?' she cut in bitingly. 'It's nothing to do with you who I marry.'

There was an unreadable expression in Jack's eyes as his glance met hers. He murmured, 'I suppose you think I've forfeited any right to be interested in your future?'

'As a matter of fact, yes, I do think that,' said Sally forcefully. What right had an ex-boy-friend to tell her the sort of man she should be marrying? She bit her lip. Perhaps she was being over-aggressive about the matter—after all, she didn't give a damn what Jack thought of Tim, did she? But the warm feelings she'd had for Jack since he'd rescued Callum Brody faded, and she glanced pointedly at her watch.

'We'd better get on,' she said coldly. 'Joyce will show you the flat and you can get dressed there. I'll run through some of the procedures in twenty minutes when I'm changed. Luckily, I've got some spare clothes I keep in the cupboard here.'

Half an hour later Sally sat down at her desk with a steaming cup of coffee and one of Joyce's home-made biscuits in front of her. Joyce had managed to get hold of Callum Brody's wife to come and pick up their little granddaughter Susy and the dog so it seemed as if the dramatic episode at the start of the day had been resolved satisfactorily. And yet, instead of feeling relieved, Sally was unsettled, and Jack's words about Tim seemed to repeat themselves in her mind.

She had to admit that on the face of it she and Tim didn't have much in common. To be honest, there had been niggling doubts when he'd first asked her to marry him. His world was so different from hers—a commercial world with hard-headed executives who lived and played hard. Although her father worked in Glasgow, they had always lived in the countryside outside the city and hers had been a privileged childhood where she'd ridden ponies, kept dogs and even sheep as pets.

But the dazzling and glamorous life Tim offered her was such a complete contrast to the past lonely six years, so full of fun—theatre first nights and dances, even flying off to France for two days. It was hard to resist such a generous and lively man. So what if neither of them felt dizzy with passion when they saw each other? They were great friends, weren't they, and that was a very important thing in relationships, wasn't it?

Tim hadn't given Sally much time to ponder on their differences. After a whirlwind courtship, they had become engaged and he'd agreed quite happily to start off their married life in Crannoch. After all, he felt he'd got a prize with Sally—he wasn't going to let a beautiful young doctor slip out of his hands!

Sally sipped her coffee absent-mindedly. A

thought crossed her mind—would Tim have another spur-of-the-moment decision like he had done with the wedding venue and decide he wanted to move somewhere more cosmopolitan? She shrugged her shoulders irritably and put her mug down so firmly on the desk that coffee spilt over onto some papers. Damn Jack McLennan and his observations for putting such a thought into her head!

She cared very much about Tim and, of course, he cared equally for her. That was all that mattered. The main thing in married life was to be together, to support each other…and if occasionally she missed the fireworks and heart-stopping thrill of attraction she'd once felt for Jack, that didn't matter, did it?

She clicked one of the icons on the screen, bringing up the list for the morning's surgery. She would not discuss her fiancé with Jack again—he had lost the right to comment on her private life a long time ago.

CHAPTER THREE

JACK tapped his pencil morosely on the desk, scowling unseeingly at the screen showing the list of patients he was to see that morning. What the hell did Sally see in Tim Langley? How could she have become engaged to him? Oh, he was probably a decent man, but he was at heart obviously someone mainly interested in business and commercial deals—did Sally really want to live in that sort of city world, where her husband's consuming interest was financial matters? Someone whose first concern was the deal he'd just pulled off and not concern for his fiancée's physical well-being after getting soaking wet in freezing waters?

A rueful grin lifted Jack's expression for a second. He'd certainly hit a nerve with Sally when he'd dared to hint that Tim Langley was less than perfect! He'd quite enjoyed doing that!

But he realised that that sort of little episode wasn't going to make for a good working relationship with Sally, and whatever he felt about her fiancé he ought to keep his mouth shut in future. It was, Jack reflected wryly, the little green monster of jealousy that was getting to him. Sally had every right to choose who she wanted to get married to.

He sighed. This job was going to be a bittersweet experience, for even if they had no future together, being near Sally made him feel more vitally alive than he had for six years.

He pressed the button to admit the first patient. If he was going to do this job properly he had to bury his personal feelings. He couldn't start his first day at the practice fulminating over a man like Tim Langley.

'Mr Angus Knightley?' he said pleasantly to the man who came in. 'I'm the locum here for a few weeks—Jack McLennan.'

Mr Knightley walked over slowly to the desk. He would have looked quite imposing but for his stooping gait and a general fragility marked by his grey complexion and dark shadows under his eyes.

He lowered himself gingerly onto the chair in front of the desk, and remarked, 'Oh, I know all about you, Doctor, and what happened this morning—saving Callum Brody from a watery grave! You're a celebrity around here now!'

'News travels fast,' remarked Jack with amusement. 'How did you know all that?'

'My daughter told me.'

'Your daughter?' asked Jack, puzzled.

Angus Knightley smiled proudly. 'The lass at Reception—Sharon. She helps that dragon of a woman, Joyce. The practice couldn't do without Sharon! She told me the other day that a man was going to do a locum job here, so I thought it would be an opportunity to have myself looked at. It's about time they had a man in the practice at last—much more satisfactory!' Then he added hastily, 'Not that I've anything against women doctors, of course!'

Jack raised a quizzical brow. 'Of course not! I hope I can help. Tell me what the trouble is.'

He waited patiently as Mr Knightley cleared

his throat and took a deep breath, as if psyching himself up to explain his symptoms. 'The...the thing is...' He stuttered a little and then said in a rush, 'It's very embarrassing, Doctor. I couldn't have let Dr Cornwell or Dr Lawson examine me...'

How often does that happen? thought Jack wryly. So many people put their embarrassment and fear before their health and then suffered the consequences of a late diagnosis. He was well used to patients' diffidence.

'Now you've managed to get yourself here, don't miss the opportunity to tell me,' he prompted gently.

Another silence as Angus grappled with the need to explain his problem and the indignity of revealing it, then he said awkwardly, 'Trouble with the...er, rear end, you know. It's damned painful.'

'You mean haemorrhoids?' Jack asked sympathetically. No wonder the man looked terrible. Although piles were the subject of much cruel humour, they were amongst the most painful of common conditions. 'How long have you been suffering with them?'

The man sighed. 'Quite a long time—a year or two, maybe. It's not the kind of thing I feel like showing a woman, and, nice though these doctors are, there's no way I'm divesting myself of my trousers!'

'It's a very common complaint, you know, but none the less painful for that. You should have put yourself out of your misery and had some advice. Every doctor sees many cases like yours.'

Mr Knightley shook his head. 'Sounds silly this, I know, but you're not from these parts and you're only here for a short time and don't know anybody. I don't want people who live here knowing my problem.'

'I can assure you that no doctor would breach any patient confidentiality outside the practice,' said Jack gently. 'Only other medical personnel who need to deal with your case would be informed.'

'So you say,' said Mr Knightley darkly. But relief at finally being able to divulge his problem had made him loquacious, more able to talk through the problem, and he added, 'I know if you have an operation for this kind of thing, it's very painful—I had an uncle who spent a fortnight in hospital unable to move for the agony he was in. I'm afraid that was one of the things that put me off coming.'

Jack smiled. 'First of all, Mr Knightley, let me reassure you—I guess it was a few years ago that your uncle had the operation, but things have moved on a lot now and techniques have evolved. After I've examined you I'll suggest what might be done to cope with the problem.'

Jack wasn't surprised that his patient was in such pain. Years of enduring his problem without help had made the problem acute—Mr Knightley definitely needed surgery. He was surprisingly upbeat at the thought of having an operation.

'I've reached the end of my tether,' he explained to Jack. 'Now I've come to see you and talked about it, I just want to get on with things. I feel better already! I'm grateful to you, Doctor, for your understanding!' He stood up and shook

Jack's hand vigorously. 'If I can help you in return, just let me know. I'm the local estate agent, so if you need any kind of property, I'm your man!'

Jack grinned and shook his head. 'Thank you, but I'm only here for a few weeks so I doubt I'll be looking for anything, although it would be tempting to do so…'

'You never know,' said Angus Knightley with an answering smile. 'You might like us so much, you'll decide to stay!'

He went out with more of a spring in his step than when he'd come in and Jack loaded the man's notes into the computer. A pity he couldn't take up Mr Knightley's offer. It was just the sort of permanent job he would have loved—everything right about it: a small community in beautiful countryside, and of course with Sally as a colleague… Pipe dreams, he thought savagely, just pipe dreams. She had her future mapped out with a man who probably had no baggage to bring to their relationship, and he, Jack, could never ask her to be part of his life—not with his background.

* * *

Sally glanced at the little clock on her desk and hoped that Mary and Bert Olsen wouldn't demand too much of her time before she had to go out on her visits. At the back of her mind she wondered how Jack had got on in his first morning—she couldn't help feeling a little ashamed of her attitude to him earlier. He'd had a baptism of fire in his new job, rescuing a man from the sea, being a hero, in fact, and perhaps he'd deserved more than the snappy way she'd talked to him after Tim had left. After all, she was the one who had asked him what he thought of Tim.

Having run tersely through the computer program and call system they used, she'd left Jack to go through the patients on his list, just telling him peremptorily to call her if he needed any help. However, now she'd had time to reflect, perhaps it might be a good idea to be a little friendlier towards him if they were to work well together. A strained atmosphere could soon permeate the whole practice. She supposed she'd have to lighten up a bit with him. She sighed, and turned her attention to the overweight couple sitting in front of her.

Mary and Bert Olsen ran a small bed-and-breakfast business in Oban, and came over to see Mary's mother, Hilda Brown, assiduously every few weeks. Although that was laudable, Sally had an uneasy feeling it wasn't just on Hilda's behalf that they came, and there was something persistent and nagging in their frequent calls to the doctor to ask how Sally thought Mrs Brown was coping. Today they had asked for an appointment to discuss Mrs Brown's situation.

Mary leaned forward and said earnestly, 'And so, Doctor, we wondered if you would assess mother for us? Since her fall two weeks ago we've been very worried.'

'She was found quite quickly. I think she slipped on a rug, didn't she? She seems to have no ill effects.'

'Ah, but it's the writing on the wall, isn't it? Mother's certainly not the woman she was—she seems quite forgetful. We have enduring power of attorney and we think it's time to put it into place. She's deteriorated, I'm sure, since we last saw her.'

Sally suspected that Hilda was frightened of them—frightened of their power to move her from the beautiful house she loved, although Sally realised it was far too big for her. Hilda had told Sally that they made frequent references to her frail health and her ability to look after herself.

'I saw Mrs Brown in the surgery two weeks ago—she seemed very capable of looking after herself then, if a little frail,' Sally observed. 'Her mind is razor sharp.'

'Oh, she puts on a good front but she's really not fit to run her own affairs—she's definitely gone downhill recently,' said Mary earnestly. 'The place is a complete tip… But, of course, it's her welfare we're thinking of, isn't it, Bob? The house is too much for her and she should be put in a home where she can be looked after properly. I'm sure she's going to do something dreadful, like leave the gas on or a tap running.'

'It's not just up to me, Mrs Olsen, even if I did think your mother needed care. Social Services would have to be brought in and another doctor. Nobody can force Mrs Brown to leave her home unless she's a danger to herself.' Sally spoke mildly—she didn't want to antagonise the Olsens. 'Why don't we offer Mrs Brown more help in the house—perhaps meals on wheels and someone to help her with a shower? Even a little help might keep her in the house for a few more years. She seems perfectly happy where she is.'

The Olsens flicked a look at each other and Bert Olson said impatiently, 'You don't understand, Dr Lawson. You don't know her as we do. Why, if anything happened to her and she fell again, we would feel it in on our conscience, wouldn't we, Mary?'

Mary nodded vigorously, and said piously, 'We'd never forgive ourselves. She'd be much better off with people looking after her twenty-four seven.'

'Falling in the elderly is certainly a danger,' agreed Sally, 'but your mother could wear an alarm pendant—if she was in trouble she'd only have to press it for help. And, of course, as I said, daily visits could be arranged by Social Services if your mother agreed.'

'I don't think that's the answer,' said Mary stubbornly. 'Won't you come and at least give us your opinion? I'm sure when you see her you'll agree with us. There must be some way she can be persuaded to move to a safer place.'

'All right,' agreed Sally. 'I'll call in today when I'm in the area—if only to put your minds at rest.'

Mary compressed her lips and stood up, pulling on her gloves. 'We think you'll agree with us, Doctor, when you see her and the state she's living in. See you later.'

Sally watched them go out. To some extent, she did sympathise with them. It was a modern phenomenon—a rising ageing population that would need looking after, often by children who were pensioners themselves, but nevertheless she did wonder if the Olsens' motives were entirely altruistic. Then she dismissed them from her mind as she walked through to the little kitchen for a restorative cup of coffee.

She hesitated for a second outside Jack's surgery. Perhaps now was the time to start mending fences—after all, they were going to be colleagues for a while and the longer she left it, the more difficult it would be. She tapped on his door, and he called out for her to come in.

When he saw it was Sally, Jack stood up, looking at her rather warily—perhaps expecting her to snap at him again, she thought with a sudden inward giggle. The reason she'd fallen for him all those years ago came back to her vividly—he was, as Sharon had so graphically said to her earlier that morning, 'the kind of man to make your knees wobble'!

His rangy figure, thick mop of russet hair and bright blue eyes had always caused women's heads to turn. Sally had been no exception, drawn to his melting looks and teasing personality from the first moment she'd met him. What a good thing she had completely got over the man years ago, because of course now she had Tim, powerful and good looking also but in a different kind of way—less raw, less exciting perhaps, less…sexy. She wondered crossly what on earth had made her use that word in comparing her fiancé to Jack—they were completely different in every way.

'You wanted something?' prompted Jack, his eyes sweeping over her slender figure now wearing a pale blue silk blouse and navy trousers, with a blue scarf knotted round her neck. His throat constricted—she looked chic and efficient and very, very desirable! 'Have you found more patients for me to see?'

His voice brought her back with a start. 'What? Oh...I just wondered if you felt like a coffee?' she asked rather breathlessly.

He nodded and smiled. 'Yep, I could do with a coffee. I think I've got to grips with this programme now, so perhaps I deserve a reward.'

There was a slightly self-conscious silence, then Sally said rather stiltedly, 'I hope things went OK?'

'No problems.'

'Good, good. After coffee I could take you on my visits to introduce you to some of our patients—there's one in particular I'd like some advice on.'

'Only too pleased to help if I can.'

A twinkle in his eyes held hers for a moment, as if he was aware that an olive branch had been offered. He followed her to the little kitchen where Sharon and Joyce were already pouring out mugs of coffee. Sharon was showing Joyce a photo in a magazine.

'Joyce, why don't you have a few highlights done, like the woman here?' Sharon was urging her. 'You need to keep that grey hair at bay—it's very ageing!'

'I like my hair to look natural, thank you,' replied Joyce tartly. 'I'll have you know I'm not spending a fortune dolling my hair up only for it to need doing again a few weeks later.'

'You giving Joyce some tips, Sharon?' asked Sally with amusement.

'She's got all sorts of mad ideas to spruce me up for this dinner I'm going to,' growled Joyce. 'Anyway, Sally, would you ring Mr Barnes from the cottage hospital? He's got a query regarding the old gentleman you asked to be admitted yesterday.'

'Sure—I'll do that this afternoon. I want Jack to come with me now to see Hilda Brown and familiarise himself a little with the area. We'll go after we've had coffee.'

As they went out they could hear Sharon saying persuasively, 'You really would look great with a feather-style cut as well, Joyce. It would be a completely new look! Why don't you?'

'I think Sharon's up against a brick wall there,' observed Jack as they got into Sally's car.

She couldn't help giggling in response.

The day had lightened and there was a pale sun filtering through the clouds as they drove towards Hilda Brown's house set up on a hill overlooking the sound between the mainland and the island. It was a view Sally never tired of as the road climbed before them, and they rose high above the glinting sea and the neat fields of wheat and pasture land under a sky of scudding clouds. Across the water, the mountains of Hersa were a blue outline against the sky. Soon they would develop a purple carpet when the heather bloomed.

'That's a beautiful sight,' murmured Jack.

'The colours are never the same—there's so much sky around. To me it's still magnificent when it's lashing with rain and there's a force-ten gale.'

They turned a corner and a herd of cows were crossing the road to be milked, forcing Sally to stop. They lapsed into silence as they waited. Funny how the inside of a car could generate a very intimate atmosphere, and it was odd how two people who had once had so much to say to each other were so tongue-tied now. She smiled as she flicked a look at Jack's legs, doubled up in front of him in her tiny car. She'd forgotten just what a tall man he was, how he dominated any room he was in. She wondered idly if he'd ever regretted his decision to break up with her. Indeed, had he ever thought of her at all during the time he was there? Of course he hadn't, she told herself scornfully, otherwise he wouldn't have taken six years to come back to Scotland.

After a few minutes she said boldly, 'So you decided not to go back to Australia because your younger brother is at university. You wanted to keep an eye on him?'

'Liam's been through rather a lot in his young life,' Jack said briefly. 'He needs what family he's got. And anyway...' he smiled faintly '...once I was back in Scotland I realised how many things I'd missed.'

'Like what?'

An unreadable expression flickered across his face then he said lightly, 'Oh, don't get me wrong, Australia's a wonderful country, but there are some things that it doesn't have...countryside like this, my old friends...' His voice trailed off and he looked out of the window at the water sparkling below them. 'I think within me I always knew I wouldn't spend my life abroad.'

The cows had been herded into the field and the road was clear. Sally changed gear and drove on. 'So you didn't find romance in Australia, then? Perhaps you were concentrating too much on your career?' she remarked with a slight edge to her voice.

A little muscle tightened in his cheek. 'Perhaps I was,' he agreed, then he said lightly, 'But maybe I just haven't been as lucky as you, Sally. How are the wedding arrangements going, by the way?'

The car bounced as Sally swerved at the last moment to avoid a pothole. 'Absolutely fine.' She smiled. 'It's all very exciting! Just rather a lot to do, that's all.'

Jack watched Sally's slim hands on the steering-wheel, and that damned vulgar engagement ring flashing in the light every time she moved the wheel. The faint scent of her perfume drifted over to him evocatively. Almost more than anything that brought back poignant memories of them together, dancing on a lawn one balmy moonlit night, his face buried in her warm neck and drinking in the light summery scent she wore... Having a drink in a pub garden after work... He flicked a look at her pert profile, silky blonde hair curving into her jawline. Six years ago they would have stopped off on the way home for a stroll over the fields— perhaps made passionate love under the sky... He sighed and gritted his teeth. He had to stop thinking like this, bringing back memories of things that could never happen again. Sally was happily engaged and he, Jack, was only a colleague of hers for a short time. He had absolutely no rights over her.

'Tell me about these patients we're going to see,' he said abruptly, his deep voice coming as a shock after the silence.

'The first call is on Hilda Brown,' Sally explained. 'She's the widow of a local solicitor and she has one married daughter, Mary Olsen. Hilda's quite frail and has angina which is well controlled. She's a very capable woman who loves living where she is, although it's a very large house—it's absolutely magnificent and called "The Chase". A short time ago she tripped over a carpet and twisted her ankle. She was found by the gardener an hour or so later—no harm done.'

'And what's your dilemma with her?'

'Her daughter and son-in-law are very keen to get her into a home—they say it's for her own good. I'm not so sure.'

'You can't force someone to go into a home unless there's evidence she needs to go for her own safety.'

'I know. I feel Mary and Bert are pressurising

me to back them up and I'd like your take on the matter. I guess you've had experience with this sort of thing in Australia?'

He nodded. 'In the remote area where I lived there was quite a problem with the elderly generation being left alone when the children had to leave the area to find work many miles away. We had to do quite a few assessments.'

'Well, the Olsens will be at the house when we go, although they live in Oban and run a B&B there.'

'You think they want you to provide a dossier that can be used to prove that Mrs Brown can't look after herself?'

Sally nodded. 'Could be. Anyway, two heads are better than one.' She changed gear and turned into a drive. 'Here we are.'

A yellow-bricked pretty house with rolling lawns stood on a slight rise, looking over to the sea, now glittering in the afternoon sun and very different from the turbulent waves of the morning. They got out of the car, and the air was crisp and fresh, the sound of a lark lifting its voice gloriously high above them.

Jack took a deep breath of pleasure and looked around him. 'What a great place,' he commented admiringly. 'As you say, rather large for one person, but if I had a place like this, I'd never want to leave it!'

Mary Olsen came out to meet them. 'Oh, I didn't realise there'd be two of you,' she said.

'This is Dr Jack McLennan, a colleague of mine,' said Sally, quickly pre-empting any objection Mary might have to his presence. 'He's had a lot of experience with elderly people, so I thought it would be helpful if he could see the situation as well.'

'I see… Well, perhaps that's for the best—two opinions would carry more weight obviously. Follow me. Mother's not in a good mood, I'm afraid.'

She led the way into a cool, dark hall surrounded by oak-panelled walls on which hung some paintings—all very valuable, Jack guessed, looking around with interest. Mrs Brown was obviously a wealthy woman. A large Labrador came bounding in to meet them, skittering to a halt on a rug when Mary shouted at him to keep still. Sally and Jack followed her into the drawing room, a magnificent room with a huge bay window overlooking sloping lawns and beyond them the view over to the island. The room itself was crammed with furniture—huge chairs, small occasional tables, a grand piano, all spilling over with papers, old mugs of tea, teetering piles of books. Magazines covered a large area of floor space, as did newspapers and photo albums, and in the bay window was a large easel with a canvas on it and brushes and paints on the window seat.

Mary looked back at the doctors with a significant smile. 'See what I mean about the place being a tip? I daren't show you the kitchen,' she said in a stage whisper.

Hilda herself was a small figure sitting in a large upright chair and wearing a funny jumble of clothes—a long skirt, comfortable boots and an old shawl thrown over her shoulders. Her white hair was shoulder length, and on her head she wore a jaunty straw hat with a ribbon around it.

'Here's Dr Lawson, Mother—I told you she

was coming. She's bought a colleague with her, Dr McLennan.'

The old lady looked at them sharply. 'I told you I didn't need any doctors coming—there's nothing wrong with me, Mary. I can't think why you're so obsessed with my health.'

'You know how worried Bert and I are about you being alone in this huge place…you're not as steady on your feet as you used to be. We think you'd feel more secure in a nice flat with a warden, or perhaps a comfy care home.'

'I've had one fall over a rug. I didn't come to any harm. I like being alone. I don't want to be secure in a "nice flat". Sounds like a prison to me. And certainly not a care home, thank you!' Hilda looked fiercely at her daughter. 'I've got my painting and the dog. I've plenty to occupy myself.'

Sally drew up a little stool and sat down by Hilda. 'I think Mary and Bert are just concerned that if anything should happen, like you having a fall, you'd be very isolated with no one near to call on.'

Bright, intelligent eyes looked steadily at

Sally. 'Ridiculous! I can cook for myself…and I've friends I can contact.'

'That's just it,' declared Mary. 'You never eat anything at all—just little bits of toast. And as for friends, they're miles away.'

Hilda ignored her. 'I can still walk down to the sea with my stick.' She turned to the two doctors. 'Mary's been harassing me for weeks to go and live somewhere else. Well, I'm not doing it, I tell you!'

Mary grimaced. 'Oh, Mother, just look at this place—it's such a mess. It's going downhill rapidly—and you're always forgetting things. One of these days you'll start a fire and the whole lot will be destroyed!'

'Well, then, I'll be forced to go somewhere else, won't I?' Hilda looked scornfully at her daughter. 'Go and put some tea on. I'll talk to the doctors privately if you don't mind!'

A flicker of annoyance crossed Mary's face as she went out. Obviously the meeting wasn't going as she'd intended!

Jack threaded his way carefully through the debris on the floor and stood in front of the canvas on the easel, looking at it for a minute in silence.

'What a fantastic picture of the sea and the island,' he murmured at last. 'Did you do this, Mrs Brown?'

Hilda smiled. 'I did, young man. Painting's my passion, and I never tire of painting the view out of that window! It's always different—the cloud formations, the colours of the hills beyond… They change constantly.' She sighed. 'I know this house is too big for me and that my legs are going, but as long as I'm able to paint I don't want to leave. I won't leave, however much that son-in-law of mine and Mary pressure me to do so!'

'Would you consider having some help?' suggested Sally. 'I know you've said you hate having people around, but if it helps you to stay in the house you love, it might be worth it.'

The old lady's face split into a broad smile. 'If it keeps Bert from getting his hands on the place, it certainly would be worth it.'

'You think he wants the house?'

Hilda Brown's expression changed and suddenly she looked very vulnerable and sad. She pulled out a handkerchief and dabbed at her eyes. 'They want me out of here, Dr Lawson. It would make a much better B&B than the one they've got—I know they're making a loss at the moment. They want to sell it and move in here.' She'd clutched Sally's hand and whispered, 'Don't let them move me, will you? I know I'm getting frailer, but it's my home…'

Above her head, Sally's and Jack's eyes met in sympathy at the old lady's plight.

'How do you know this, Mrs Brown?' Jack said gently. He moved away from the window and came to sit in a chair by Mrs Brown.

'I've heard them arguing about money and Bert saying that this house would be a good upmarket B&B. I know Mary's my daughter, but we've never really hit it off—she was totally spoilt by her father and always wants her own way. I've tried to be fair to her, set her up with the house in Oban, but they ran it badly, and now they see this house as a more attractive proposition, but I'm not ready to leave yet just to convenience them!'

'Then there's no reason why you should,' declared Sally. 'Don't you agree, Dr McLennan?'

He leaned forward in his chair and held Hilda's hand gently in his, his smile reassuring, and Sally watched him, remembering his deft touch with patients from their A and E days.

'I'm sure you could live here for many years. There's all kinds of help that would make life much easier for you. For example, why not have meals on wheels? It is important that you eat regularly, you know, and it would save you the bother of making something for yourself. And then there's an alarm pendant, which you wear round your neck and can press any time you need help.'

Hilda looked at the two doctors wryly. 'Old age is a damn nuisance,' she said, then she sighed and relaxed back in her chair. 'Perhaps I will have some help. Would you tell my daughter that I've agreed to your suggestions? Let it come straight from the horse's mouth, as it were!' An impish smile spread over her face. 'And now let me guess, Dr Lawson. I've been looking at that ring on your finger—is this young man your fiancé? I must say you two make a very handsome couple—just right for each other I'd say!'

Sally and Jack looked briefly at each other, and Sally felt her cheeks redden. 'Oh, no, Dr McLennan's not engaged—you're quite fancy-free, aren't you?' she said, quickly turning to Jack with a forced little laugh.

'And Dr Lawson's getting married in a few weeks to someone who isn't a doctor so I'm not in the picture at all,' added Jack lightly.

The old lady looked keenly at them both for a second. 'Ah, I'm sorry to get it so wrong. As you young people say, I must have felt vibes that weren't there!'

Sally fumbled for her key to open the front door, longing to get into the house and have a light supper in front of the fire. Normally she would have looked forward to the prospect of discussing wedding arrangements with Tim, but it had been a very long day, starting with the rescue of Callum Brody and culminating in rather an uncomfortable episode with Mary and Bert Olsen.

Sally had been glad of Jack's input, firm but pleasant and not about to be browbeaten into making the decision the Olsens wanted, and it had been good to have his support in her assessment of Mrs Brown. Her daughter had not agreed with their opinion that Hilda was going to be fine in her own home if she had some help, but as Jack had pointed out, in the end it was Hilda, the doctor and Social Services' decision where she would live.

Sally flung down her medical bag on the sofa and took off her coat, then noticed a note on the little table by the telephone.

'Sally, sweetie, sorry I'll have to change the arrangements for tonight. I waited for a while here, but I've had to go back urgently to Glasgow and tidy up a few points regarding this deal I've been negotiating. In the meantime, would you contact my secretary, Rita, about putting in hand some fresh invitations with the new venue—Carswell Towers—on them?

We'll need about fifty more than the original number. You only get married once so why not do it in real style and give all our friends a day to remember? Text me if you need more information. See you, Tim.'

Sally sat down heavily on the sofa and stared ahead of her. The people he wanted to invite weren't really friends—just business acquaintances, people she neither knew nor cared about. But Tim, in his expansive way, had insisted that it would be foolish to leave them out. It was a perfect opportunity to build contacts in his world, he'd explained.

She got up and wandered over to the little bay window of her lounge and looked over the now tranquil sea to Hersa. Six years ago she and Jack had talked about marriage—he had suggested they have a quiet wedding in her home village with just immediate family. They would have a simple meal in the local pub and go on a walking holiday in the Trossachs. It had sounded ideal. She sighed. That wasn't Tim's style, and it was no good wishing it was. And of course her parents were looking forward to all the celebrations—the more the merrier, her father always said.

Sally leaned against the windowsill, pressing her hot forehead against the cool glass. It had to be because she was tired, but suddenly she realised that her excitement over her wedding had changed somewhat. For whatever reason, she had a strange apprehension, like a small cloud, hanging over the happy day. It was as if a steamroller was coming towards her and, whatever was done, it couldn't be stopped.

Then she flicked her hair impatiently from her face and went into the kitchen, pouring herself a glass of water. These sorts of thoughts were ridiculous—of course she couldn't wait to get married to Tim. She was just having a little blip that thousands of brides experienced.

Perhaps it was the shock of meeting Jack so unexpectedly that seemed to have unsettled her in some way, disturbed old forgotten wounds, triggered a feeling of dissatisfaction with her relationship with Tim—and that was completely ridiculous! She had an exciting new life mapped out before her, and of course she couldn't wait to begin it with Tim!

CHAPTER FOUR

'SO THIS is the final fitting, Sally. Let me do the dress up at the back…there! It fits perfectly. Now just look at yourself—you look stunning!'

Sally turned towards the long mirror and silently surveyed her reflection. The long white lace dress clung to her slender frame, its scalloped neckline showing the discreet swell of her breasts and emphasising her slim waist, as it swirled to the floor in soft folds from the hip. Little beads of crystal were sewn round the neck and randomly over the lace—the dress looked elegant and very expensive.

'Well?' demanded Sue, who'd made the dress. 'Don't you agree you look wonderful in it?'

Sally smiled. 'It's certainly very flattering but I won't be able to put on an ounce of weight before the wedding!'

'Your groom will faint with delight when he

sees you coming up the aisle,' declared Sue. 'Remember, though, he mustn't see you in it before the Big Day—it's very bad luck!'

The Big Day! Sally wondered if all brides felt as apprehensive as she did before they got married. She had hardly seen Tim over the last few days as it seemed the business deal was proving more complicated than he'd thought and he'd had little time to get over to Crannoch. She looked at herself in the mirror again. Suddenly the dress seemed rather constricting—dare she say it, like a straitjacket? Putting on the wedding dress emphasised the fact that there could be no turning back now—she had to go through with the wedding.

'Don't look so worried, Sally. Remember it is a wedding we're planning here, not a funeral.' Sue laughed. She looked assessingly at Sally. 'You do look a little pale, darling…you've obviously been working too hard! You need looking after as well as your patients, you know!'

'I'm OK. A few sleepless nights, I'm afraid. Too much to think about, I expect.'

There'd been loads of texts about the new

venue, the caterers Tim wanted to hire and the photographers he wanted to book—apparently he was keen that they have their wedding featured in several magazines. It was as if he was determined to make as big a show as possible, and of course he wanted everything to be just right, thought Sally.

'We're going to remember this day for the rest of our lives, Sally,' he'd said to her. 'And so are all our guests! Any difficulties, ask Rita—she'll be happy to help.'

Tim's secretary was certainly very efficient and Sally had been more than relieved to let her do the chasing up of the many people who were apparently necessary to organise a wedding. Rita had loads of good suggestions and advice. As she told Sally, she had done the 'wedding thing', as she put it, although she was divorced now, and knew all the pitfalls. It was she who had suggested that Sue should come over from Glasgow to Crannoch to make final adjustments to the wedding dress to save Sally time. Sue had a beautiful gown shop in the city, selling not only bridalwear but ballgowns and cocktail wear, and she and Sally had become friendly over the past few months.

Sue was looking at a photo of Tim on the mantelpiece—it had been taken on one of his friend's yachts on a blowy day, and he looked tanned, his hair tousled.

'Wow! What a handsome couple you'll make. Your fiancé's drop-dead gorgeous!' she remarked, impressed. 'Are there any more where he comes from?'

Sally laughed. 'He's got a brother, but he's married.'

She looked at the photo herself. It was a good one, showing Tim with his open, engaging look—even on paper his image seemed to fizz with energy. She was a lucky girl, no doubt, to get someone so competent, generous and ambitious. Unbidden, Jack's words suddenly came back to her. *He isn't the kind of man I thought you'd go for.* How wrong he was, Sally thought crossly. Tim was everything she wanted, he was popular at his work and her parents were delighted she was marrying him. Happiness at last for their darling daughter. What more could she want?

She gave a little twirl and looked again at herself in the mirror. Sue really had done a wonderful job on the dress, and yet she felt uneasy, as if the role of beautiful bride in white didn't sit easily on her. Then she reassured herself that when she saw Tim that evening her worries about the organisation of the wedding would fade—he was coming over from Glasgow and taking her out for a meal. It had been ages since she'd seen him; in fact, lately she'd felt that she came a poor second to his business commitments.

Sue watched her indulgently and smiled. 'I haven't met a girl who looked better in one of my dresses,' she remarked with satisfaction. 'Give up your day job and come and model for me!'

Sally gave a rather forced laugh. 'It's not hard to look good in one of your creations. I can't thank you enough for all your trouble, Sue—it's a fairy-tale dress! Go and make some coffee for us both while I drool over it for a minute more before it's put away!'

The doorbell rang as Sue went to the kitchen. 'Shall I get it?' she called out.

'If you would,' said Sally, turning in front of the mirror, trying to dispel the peculiar uneasiness she felt about wearing the dress.

Mumbled voices came from the hallway and then Sue called out, 'It's your colleague, Jack… he needs to speak to you urgently about work. Do you mind if he comes in?'

'What?' Sally flew round, eyes wide with embarrassment. 'No—wait a moment! I'll just take off the dress and put something else on…'

She certainly didn't want Jack McLennan to see her in her wedding dress—not the man she'd once loved so much, the man she'd hoped to marry once upon a time…It was too personal, too intimate for anyone to look at, except Tim and her guests on the day of the wedding.

It was too late. The door opened and Jack stepped into the room. Two pairs of eyes held each other for a second—his in astonishment, hers almost defiantly. There was a moment's silence, and his gaze travelled slowly over her. The shocked expression on his face quickly mutated to one of open admiration.

'Wow!' he murmured. 'You look amazing, Sally!'

Why did she feel so self-conscious in front of this man's scrutiny? She was proud of the way she looked, wasn't she? Suddenly she changed her mind about not wanting Jack to see her in her wedding dress. He may not love her anymore, but she knew she looked pretty good and perhaps he'd feel the slightest pang at seeing what he'd missed all those years ago! In some childish way Sally wanted to pay him back for the heartache she'd suffered when he'd left her high and dry—to show him that although he'd dumped her so unceremoniously, she wasn't crushed. She had someone who loved her and she was deliriously happy—wasn't she? Something devilish inside her made her want to taunt him.

'You think I look OK, then, as the blushing bride?' she said almost coquettishly, looking at him under her eyelashes, waiting expectantly for his answer when he didn't reply for a second.

Jack's eyes seemed to darken, but he grinned and said with a casual throw-away line, 'Oh, your groom can have absolutely no complaints—he's one lucky guy.'

Why did she feel that little frisson of disappointment? Sally knew he felt nothing for her now—and of course that feeling was mutual—but he might have been more fulsome in his praise of how she looked! Surely she merited a little more than 'Your groom can have absolutely no complaints...' It sounded as if he was describing an efficient personal assistant or secretary!

'So what was it you wanted to see me about?' she said rather stiffly.

Jack's expression changed and he looked grim. 'I'm afraid this isn't a social call. There's been a multiple pile-up at the lights on the main road and there are several serious injuries. There's a red alert at the hospital. It's stretched to breaking point because of another serious incident. They couldn't get hold of you, but I knew you were here during your lunch hour and said I'd contact you on my way to the hospital.'

A shocked intake of breath came from Sally. 'And they want us both in, I suppose?' she said, suddenly feeling slightly ashamed that all she was concerned about were her bruised feelings! She grimaced. 'God, I hope I'm up to it. It's been some time since I've done any A and E work.'

'Don't worry, you'll be fine, just as good as you used to be when you worked in Casualty.' He smiled encouragingly at her worried face, his eyes dancing reassuringly into hers.

'But that was six years ago,' she squeaked.

'You'll slip back into it as if you've never been away,' he assured her firmly.

She sighed. 'I hope you're right. I'll follow you as quickly as possible. In all the years I've worked here I haven't ever known the hospital call on local GPs.'

'It's pretty much a chaotic situation, I believe,' said Jack. 'I'll drive there now. It'll take about a quarter of an hour for the paramedics to sort everything out at the crash scene anyway so you've a little leeway.'

He looked for a second at Sally standing slim and elegant in the beautiful bridal dress then he turned abruptly and walked briskly out of the cottage. God, he thought bitterly as he crossed the road to his car, how hard it had been to sound so casual when he'd really been knocked sideways by Sally's beauty in her wedding gown. It had twisted his heart to see how she would have looked six years ago for him if they had married…

He got into the car and revved the engine angrily. There were so many 'if onlys' in his life— if only he hadn't been born into his particular family, if only he'd turned a blind eye to what had happened within it… He gazed sadly ahead of him, and then, as so often happened to him, a terrible and graphic image appeared vividly in his mind's eye. A bike spinning on the road, a girl hurtling into the air and landing on the car that had hit her. In his head he heard her scream and then the sound stop abruptly. There was a brief silence followed by the roar of the car engine as it accelerated and drove off into the distance. The girl was left alone, motionless on the road.

He pushed the car into gear and moved off. Every time that vivid memory occurred it reminded him why he could never ask any girl to marry him, and that he too could end up like his father.

Sue came into the little living room and handed Sally a coffee. 'Sounds like you're needed in a hurry,' she remarked wryly. 'Let me help you off with the dress. I'll put it away and lock up for you if you want to get off. I'll put the key back through the letter-box.'

'Thanks, Sue. I'll see you on the big day. You will be there to help me and the bridesmaids get ourselves ready?'

'Wouldn't miss it for the world.' Sue smiled. 'And don't worry about anything—you'll be a perfect bride!'

It was lashing with rain, and Sally peered through the windscreen and the swishing window wipers as she drove cautiously to the hospital. It had to be a major incident indeed for the hospital to call in local doctors, she thought, her brain spinning with anxiety, hoping that Jack was right and that she would slip back into it.

A large crowd had gathered behind a cordon placed by the police, and Sally could see the scene as she drove by on the other side of the square. Several vehicles were locked together in a hideous tangle, one probably having skidded into another as it crossed the lights, causing multiple collisions behind it. Broken glass and twisted metal littered the road and three ambulances and a fire engine were at the scene. Police and firemen were trying to clear the road of some of the debris to let paramedics get to the injured, and one of them came towards her with his hand up.

'Sorry, madam, I'll have to ask you to turn back. We need to keep the road free for emergency vehicles.'

Sally leaned out of the window. 'It's OK. I'm a doctor—I've been asked to help at the hospital.'

The man nodded and waved her through. 'There's going to be plenty of patients for you to see,' he said grimly.

'Any idea what caused it, officer?' she asked as she slipped the car into gear.

The man shook his head. 'It's not official, but I hear that some damn fool with too much booze inside him jumped the lights—couldn't wait ten seconds for them to change.'

The old hospital at Crannoch hadn't been built for large emergencies and now consisted of hastily erected wings stuck on either side of the old Victorian facade. Every year vague promises had been made to have a new hospital built but so far nothing had materialised. Sally ran towards the A and E entrance, now crowded with ambulances and paramedics unloading figures on trolleys, and her heartbeat quickened as it always had when she'd been a junior doctor about to deal with an emergency situation.

A few grim-faced policemen stood patiently waiting by the reception desk to interview those patients who weren't too badly injured, trying to keep out of the way of the staff. Sally pushed her way through the melee in the corridor and went to the desk, where a harassed-looking nurse handed her some green scrubs.

'Dr Hallam's directing everything from Sister's office,' she explained. 'It's a bit chaotic at the moment, with two majors happening at once.'

The nurse wasn't exaggerating, thought Sally, as she dodged trolleys and oxygen cylinders being wheeled up and down the corridor. Everything looked in turmoil but she knew that there would be organisation under the seeming chaos, and triaging of patients would ensure that the most urgent of cases would be seen to first.

In Sister's office, Dr Hallam looked up from the little crowd of people round him. 'Ah, Sally, I'm grateful you could make it—we need all hands to the pump today.'

Sally had met Dr Hallam, the A and E consultant, at a few meetings in the past. He was a short bluff man with a reassuring manner, and usually nothing seemed to faze him.

'Our team is dealing with the RTA on the main road and we've a few fractures—at least one of them compound, as well as head injuries, etcetera. I believe Jack McLennan's your colleague? He's in the small theatre with a seriously injured lady and as you know him, perhaps you'd go and help him do all the usual—obs, bloods, X-rays...'

Funny how things came full circle, reflected Sally as she pushed open the door of the small theatre. The smell, the bustling atmosphere brought back quite vividly the time she and Jack had worked together in a similar scenario. It was like rewinding a film, seeing his familiar tall figure bending over the patient in the bed. There was a difference, of course: now they were merely professional colleagues—not lovers.

There was a young nurse—very young, Sally noted, standing by Jack. She was looking round-eyed and nervously at the patient, who obviously had severe injuries. Jack was sounding the patient's chest and straightened up when he heard Sally come in, just a slight rise of one eyebrow to acknowledge his colleague.

'Dr Lawson, this is Lucy, a student nurse brought over from the medical ward. She's filling in for the shortages.' His eyes looked meaningfully into Sally's. 'Lucy's not had any experience yet in Casualty.'

And, therefore, is as nervous as a cat on a hot tin roof, thought Sally. She sympathised with the girl. It was very daunting to be flung into a dramatic situation with no experience—it would be a steep learning curve.

'You'll soon find your feet,' she said bracingly, while looking assessingly at the woman on the bed and flicking a look at the screen above the patient's head recording her vital signs: read-outs of her oxygen levels, pulse rate and blood pressure.

Lucy gulped and stammered. 'I…I hope so.'

'This is our patient, Geraldine Foster,' Jack said without preamble. 'She's a lady of fifty-four and she was trapped under the rear of a bus.' His voice dropped slightly. 'Suspected broken femur and a compound fracture of her tibia. We'll need venous access and detailed X-rays, of course.'

Geraldine was grey-faced and shaking, in deep shock. A temporary dressing was over a cut on her cheek, oozing blood, and her left leg looked contorted. The paramedics had already put a collar round her neck and she was hooked up to a drip. Sally gave a little grimace of sympathy—the pain from her injuries would be intense.

The woman stared wordlessly up at Jack and he patted her hand gently. Everyone knew how important physical contact was in bringing the patient reassurance and lowering their anxiety level in the alien situation of the hospital. An hour ago this woman would have been going about her daily life as usual but suddenly and dramatically she'd been catapulted into a world of strangers, machinery and pain, and precious little time to adjust to it emotionally.

'Don't worry, Geraldine,' he said softly. 'You're in safe hands. We're going to find out exactly where you've injured yourself—you'll have X-rays very soon and possibly a scan…' He turned to indicate Sally. 'This is my colleague, Dr Lawson…she'll be getting some blood from you so that we know your blood group and lots of other information.' He grinned down at her. 'She's a regular vampire, but you won't feel a thing.'

The woman made a brave attempt to smile then groaned. 'God…the pain. Can you do something for the pain, Doctors?'

'I've got something that'll make you feel better than a glass of champagne in a minute.' Sally smiled, pulling on a pair of latex gloves, and testing the syringe before injecting the pain-killer. 'This is diamorphine and you'll feel a new woman soon.' She looked up at Jack. 'Five milligrams?'

'Yup—that should be fine.' He added quietly, 'She's very shocked—we'd better keep an eye on that drip to keep her fluids up. I'll go and contact X-Ray and get some portable films done here before the orthopaedic surgeon comes down.'

While Sally chatted to Geraldine, trying to talk her through the terrible experience she'd just had, she took blood from the woman's arm and transferred it to several ampoules to be checked for haemoglobin, urea and electrolytes.

She turned to Lucy and said, 'As you probably know, shock can send the chemistry of the blood haywire, so we need to know what's happening. We also need it to be cross-matched in case of a later transfusion.' She labelled the ampoules and handed them to Lucy. 'Take these down to the path lab. I've labelled them as urgent, so hopefully we'll get the results back very soon.'

'Do you remember anything about the accident?' Sally asked Geraldine gently as Lucy bolted out of the room with the bloods, eager to be doing something.

'Not really—it all happened so quickly,' whispered the woman. A flicker of worry crossed her face and she struggled to haul herself up slightly. 'Oh, no!' she panted. 'I've just remembered—I was going to a new job up the coast. What will the old lady think of me? She'll not know I've been in a crash.'

Jack came back into the room and put a restraining hand on Geraldine's shoulder. 'Whoa, there! No good trying to leap up at the moment. Just lie back and try and relax.' His eyes smiled down at the woman. 'And if you can enjoy our ministrations, so much the better!'

'If you tell us where you were going, I'll get someone to contact them and explain what's happened,' said Sally.

Geraldine looked miserably up at her. 'It's such a lovely job too—I was really looking forward to it. A beautiful house. I was going to help the old lady there—be a sort of daily housekeeper. She's called Hilda Brown.'

Sally and Jack looked at each other in surprise. 'We happen to know that lady,' said Jack.

'We'll certainly put her in the picture and I know she'll be most understanding. Perhaps she'll be able to get temporary help until you can start work again.'

The woman shook her head and said mournfully, 'I don't expect I'll be able to work for a long time.'

A porter arrived to take Geraldine down to X-Ray and Sally and Jack watched as she was carefully wheeled away.

'She's right,' commented Jack. 'She'll be a long time recovering, but perhaps she was lucky to get away with only being injured. I suppose someone was trying to jump the lights.'

Sally stopped writing up the woman's notes for a minute. 'The policeman I saw thought it could be a drunken driver that caused it,' she remarked.

'Then I hope they throw the book at him,' said Jack, real venom in his voice. 'And they should be made to see the consequences of their actions as well—the broken bodies and lives!'

Sally was surprised at the viciousness of his tone. Accidents caused by drunken driving weren't unusual. And it wasn't that it didn't mean anything—it just helped to numb emotions slightly so that the victims could be dealt with professionally.

'I know it's ghastly, but depressingly it seems to be quite frequent.'

Briefly, an expression of great sadness seemed to flicker across his face then he gave a wry shrug. 'Sorry, it's just one of those scenarios that really hits a nerve. RTAs can ruin too many lives. Look at Mrs Foster. How long will it take her and the other people involved, mentally and physically, to get over her accident—it could be years. And when the accident's caused by someone drinking too much, it's pure selfishness. There's no excuse.'

He was right, of course, but, then, there were so many things to get worked up about in Casualty—drugs, cruelty, violence. The list was endless.

Dr Hallam poked his head round the door. 'Don't go away, you two. We've got a critical patient coming in—can you go to the resuscitation room, check it's set up for another patient? There's already two patients in there, but the crash team's on its way.'

A trolley was being pushed at speed along the corridor, a large inert figure lying on it, and as he was pushed into the room, a tell-tale stain of blood was spreading across the blanket that covered him. The patient was haemorrhaging, his face ashen.

Jack swore softly, as the bed was pushed near the monitors. 'This is going to be touch and go.'

He called out to an orderly, 'Get in touch with the blood bank, and we need an anaesthetist to intubate.' Then he looked up at Sally, his eyes narrow and cold, and muttered harshly and succinctly, his voice just audible over the hum of monitoring machines and the general noise of nursing staff in the room, 'This man's been drinking heavily—I can smell it on him.'

Then he got on with what he had to do, his face impassive, but the implication was obvious—he thought this man was the cause of the accident.

'Not up to us to assume anything, Jack, is it?' she murmured, surprised that he should even bother voicing his thoughts.

'I was just making a medical observation,' he snapped tersely.

He pulled back the blanket covering the man and Sally heard Lucy draw in her breath in horror. The huge theatre light above the victim shone brightly on the vivid red blood that seeped from the victim's thigh.

Sally gulped in shock. God, was she up to it? Could she cope? She flicked a look at Jack, his face grim and absorbed, concentrating on the matter in hand, doing his best, whatever his private thoughts were, to save the man. Then her adrenalin kicked in and she had no time to think. She found herself sliding into the automatic mode she been trained to follow when she'd worked in Casualty years ago.

Lucy looked almost as white-faced as the patient. 'I…I don't have any experience of this sort of thing,' she whispered.

'Then this is a very good time to get some— look, listen and learn.' Sally's voice was brisk as she set up a saline drip—the only nurse available was Lucy and she seemed unable to move. There wasn't time to show this girl anything slowly, and she hoped Lucy would be able to cope. As Sally tried to find a vein to get a line in, she talked through the procedures concisely and calmly, hoping it would concentrate Lucy's mind on the patient and not on her own feelings.

'First off, we have to stop the bleeding. If too much blood is lost from the body, the organs will go into irreversible shock and we'll lose the patient. Pass me that artery clip, please.'

She pointed to the instrument she wanted on the instrument tray, and with a shaking hand Lucy handed it to her.

'We must keep the airway clear,' continued Sally as she tried the tricky business of getting the clip on the damaged artery. 'And then we have to replace the fluids. These are the three basics in a haemorrhaging situation—the essential points to saving a life—simple but essential before anything else.'

There was a sudden thump behind her and Lucy collapsed to the floor just as the crash team arrived. There was no time to feel sorry for the girl, just a flurry of activity as people surrounded the body on the bed, putting a suction catheter in place, each person attending to a different task to keep the man alive.

The anaesthetist started to intubate the patient, protecting the airway in case his breathing was compromised, and Jack was listening to the man's chest.

'What are his obs?' he asked.

'BP eighty over thirty and falling, pulse a hundred and thirty five.' The anaesthetist's voice was terse, snapping out the list of observations. 'Glasgow coma scale of 3, unresponsive. There's an internal bleed somewhere—he's very hypovolaemic. He needs to get to Theatre as soon as we've done what we can here. See what the bed situation is in ICU.' He turned round and said irritably to one of the orderlies, 'Can you get this nurse out of here before we all fall over her?'

Lucy was hauled out rather unceremoniously, and the rest of the room's efforts were concentrated on the man whose life was ebbing away on the bed. It was touch and go, but the treatment was in essence fairly simple—they had to get enough fluids in him to reverse the shock his body had gone into and keep his vital organs working. Sally felt hot and sticky under her hospital scrubs, suddenly conscious of her aching back and legs and the heat of the room. At last Jack straightened up.

'I think he'll be OK,' he said rather wearily. 'His BP's on the way up and his pulse is stable. Let's get him to Theatre to see where this internal bleed is.'

Gradually the rooms emptied of people as patients were transferred to the main wards, ICU or operating theatres to have broken limbs reset or internal injuries investigated.

Talk about an exhausting afternoon! Sally felt as if a tight band had been round her forehead, and her head thumped with the tension of dealing with a situation she hadn't encountered for a few years. But there was also a sense of elation and satisfaction—they'd helped to save many lives over the past few hours and incredibly she felt she'd managed to keep up.

She wandered outside to a small garden area, away from the diesel-ridden air where the ambulances drew up. The rain had stopped and in the garden the air smelt of fresh grass and newly turned earth and a bird was singing a late afternoon snatch of song. She stretched her stiff limbs then sank down on a bench, closing her eyes and breathing in deeply.

'Feeling the pace?' said a familiar voice. 'It's hard when you're not used to it, isn't it?'

Her eyes flew open to see Jack standing in front of her, a wry smile on his face.

She said drily, 'I don't know how we used to do it—being a GP seems extremely staid after the last few hours!'

He grinned. 'Something rather exciting about it, though—actually saving some lives and seeing what happens at the other end of the spectrum, working as a team.'

He sat down beside her, longs legs crossed in front of him, and leaned back with his arm along the back of the bench behind her. He was silent for a second then said quietly, 'Quite like the old days really. I'd forgotten how tense it could be—what a roller-coaster ride...'

He turned in his seat and looked at her, putting out a hand to brush aside a lock of her hair from her forehead, his finger trailing down her jaw. They both sat very still, their eyes holding each other's in a sudden mutual memory of adrenalin-fuelled dramas six years ago. The blue of his eyes seemed to intensify and his face softened.

'We made a good team just now,' he murmured. 'But, then, we always worked well together, didn't we?'

'That's true,' she whispered, her throat unaccountably dry, her pulse suddenly racing as she felt his touch.

He looked just like he had then, Sally reflected. Not much older, and incredibly attractive, blue eyes smiling at her, thick hair tousled… Suddenly she felt an unbearable urge to kiss him once more, feel again his firm mouth on hers, demanding, passionate. She closed her eyes for a second, willing back the years. How many times in the past after a gruelling shift in Casualty had they gone home to wind down and make love on the floor in front of the fire? Disturbingly, she almost felt the texture of the soft carpet they'd lain on, the heat from the glowing logs on their bare bodies, and Jack holding her in his arms, his lips finding hers and kissing her, softly at first, and then more demandingly… Even now she felt her body responding to his nearness, every nerve tingling in anticipation of his touch—as she never did with Tim.

She stood up abruptly, furious with herself. She mustn't forget that this was the man who had betrayed her, dumped her unceremoniously and got as quickly out of her life as he could—he'd left her bereft and heartbroken for a long time. How dared Jack bring up memories of their time years ago? It was unsettling and completely inappropriate for her to be having erotic thoughts about anyone other than Tim!

She flicked a look at her watch. 'I must fly,' she said coldly, starting to walk quickly towards the car park. 'Tim's taking me out for a special dinner tonight, and I want to soak in a bath first.'

But as she drove off, her emotions as chaotic as colours in a kaleidoscope, guilt swept over her and bewilderment. Surely if she loved Tim, she shouldn't be feeling any sort of attraction for Jack? Why the hell was she allowing herself to feel this way with him when she was engaged, for heaven's sake? Jack wasn't part of her life now and she felt nothing but scorn for the way he'd treated her…and yet he seemed to enter her thoughts more and more.

CHAPTER FIVE

LYING in a steaming bath with a glass of white wine to sip, Sally stretched luxuriously in the soapy water and pushed thoughts of the chaotic afternoon out of her head. At last she was seeing Tim after a few days apart, and this would chase away this stupid reaction she'd had to Jack—she needed to talk to him face to face, not just by texts, to discuss their plans. Over the past few weeks getting together had seemed difficult. They hadn't had an intimate conversation for ages—an intimate anything, she reflected wistfully. They were both very busy people, of course, working in different places, but the fact was that the more involved the wedding plans became, the less close they seemed to be…and did a little voice whisper to her that the less she missed him?

How stupid she was being—getting het-up

about what should be a happy occasion! She hauled herself reluctantly out of the bath and dressed quickly in some navy silk palazzo pants and a soft pink silk blouse that she knew Tim liked, then brushed her hair until it shone, thick and glossy round the curve of her neck. She leant forward to inspect her face in the mirror and sighed. Her eyes had dark shadows under them and she looked pale and washed out. That's what a crazy afternoon in Casualty did for you, she thought wryly. Then she heard the front door open and knew Tim had arrived. He was standing in the little sitting room, his ear glued to his mobile phone.

'Tim, darling!' she cried, running towards him, flinging her arms round him and kissing him enthusiastically, forcing herself to be affectionate and welcoming.

He gave her a quick, rather absent hug with one arm, muttered something into the mobile phone in the other hand, and, smiling down at her, gently disengaged himself.

'Hello, sweetie,' he said. He looked slightly discomfited—a rare thing for a man as confident as he was. 'Actually, I know you won't mind, but Rita's come along too—I thought it would help if she was in on our discussions about the wedding as she's got all the info.'

It was then Sally noticed Tim's secretary, Rita, standing behind him, holding a bulging brief-case, a rather embarrassed smile on her face. She stepped forward, a picture of chic and efficiency in a fitted black dress and maroon linen jacket, not a hair out of place.

'I don't mean to intrude, but it just seemed a good opportunity to get you both together,' Rita said apologetically. 'We could run over all the items so much easier face to face and Tim suggested it would save time if I came with you for a quick meal—and then disappeared, of course!'

Sally bit her lip. It wasn't quite the evening she had been looking forward to so much, and Tim should have mentioned it to her. She felt a wave of irritation and resentment flash through her—she was beginning to feel like an outsider in these wedding arrangements!

She swallowed hard, trying to keep her irritation under control. 'So it's to be a business meeting, is it, Tim? And where are we going to eat?'

'I thought Drumrig Castle. It's a good sort of place to discuss things—not too dark and gloomy, like some of the places round here.'

And not the place for a romantic evening, thought Sally rather sadly. The evening she'd anticipated had suddenly become flat and the last thing she wanted to discuss were wedding plans with an outsider present. She couldn't understand why Tim had wanted Rita to come along, however efficient the woman was.

Sally sat silently in the car as Tim and Rita chatted brightly to each other on the way to Drumrig Castle. They seemed to have lots to say to each other, discussing work at the office, alluding to people and places she didn't know, laughing at in-jokes to do with work. In fact, she reflected, Tim had more to say to Rita than he did to her…and Rita had had so much input into the wedding it was almost as if it was her day, not Sally's.

Coldly and analytically Sally began to dissect her relationship with Tim—would a man who loved his fiancée manage to see her just twice in the last few weeks, although they only worked an hour apart? If he wanted to have an intimate and rare evening with her, would he invite his damn secretary along to discuss the finer points of their wedding? Sally rubbed her forehead tiredly with her fingers. Perhaps she was wrong, but she definitely got the feeling that the fizz had gone out of her relationship with Tim, and rightly or wrongly he didn't want to be alone with her.

She thought wistfully of how she'd felt when she and Jack had been lovers—she'd only have to see him at the end of the corridor to feel dizzy with desire, her whole body quickening, longing to feel his arms around her and his hard body pressed to her soft curves. What risks they'd taken! Her lips curved into a smile, remembering covert passionate embraces in sluice rooms, store cupboards, Jack even locking them both into a small conference room, having first put the 'Meeting in Progress' sign up on the door!

'It's not a lie,' he'd said virtuously, pulling

her towards him. 'We are having a meeting—a very interesting meeting…' And then his lips had taken hers in a gentle kiss that had become more demanding, and in the throes of passion they'd found themselves with almost nothing on when someone had knocked at the door! That, she thought with an inward giggle, had been one of their more exciting moments. Never had she dressed so quickly in her life!

She sighed softly. Wasn't that what love should be? Oblivious to everything around you except the person you loved? And yet now…now she was supposed to be getting married in a few weeks to a man she seldom saw and to whom it seemed she had little to say. She leaned back in the car and closed her eyes, a horrible feeling of panic coming over her. What the hell was she doing? If Tim wasn't madly in love with her, then she suddenly realised her feelings for him too had died down to very lukewarm ones.

The car swung into the car park of the Drumrig Castle Hotel and they all got out, scrunching their way across the gravel to the entrance.

'I'll have to go back to Glasgow tonight,' remarked Tim. 'I have to be up so early for a meeting that it wouldn't be worth stopping here.'

Not worth stopping? Sally gave a sad little shrug of her shoulders. Surely that said it all. Perhaps they were about to make the biggest mistake of their lives.

The room was large and flashy with huge chandeliers overhead and stiff tropical flowers on each table. They sat down for a drink first, and Sally felt the beginnings of a hammering headache that stayed with her throughout a meal she didn't really feel like. And all the time it was she who felt like the outsider, a gooseberry interfering with a nice evening out for Tim and Rita.

'Have a good evening last night, then?' Jack looked speculatively at Sally over the rim of his mug as he sipped his coffee, noting her white face and the large dark circles under her eyes. 'Go anywhere nice?'

Sally didn't look up from slitting open an envelope. 'Very nice, thank you. And, yes, it was a good meal,' she replied tersely, running her eye over a letter from the health authority about some new directives.

She actually wasn't reading the text of the letter, she was thinking what a horrible evening it had been and how she hadn't been able to wait for it to end. Eventually she had pleaded a bad headache and asked Tim to take her home immediately after they'd eaten.

From the moment she'd conceived the idea that Tim was more attuned to Rita than her, she'd noticed many other things—like the way he'd helped Rita on with her jacket and given an absent-minded affectionate squeeze of her shoulders when he'd done so; the way he'd leaned forward over the table towards her, asking her opinion over something, holding her eyes in his for a second too long—or so it appeared to Sally.

At first she'd thought she was being paranoid, reading things into gestures that probably hadn't been intended. It wasn't even that Rita flirted with Tim. It was just that the two of them had a very easy relationship—they seemed comfortable in each other's company. That in itself was not a signal that Tim was having an affair with Rita, but it seemed to highlight how distant she herself and Tim had become over the last few weeks, just when they should have been at their closest.

Sally didn't dislike Rita—in fact, she rather liked her and admired her polished looks and bright personality. It was ironic, she thought, that Rita and Tim seemed to make a very well-matched couple. And when Tim dropped Sally off, both of them expressing concern at her headache, she had watched them drive off together back to Glasgow and been surprised at how unemotional she felt.

What had gone wrong with their relationship? At first it had all been so exciting, being engaged, being taken to exciting places…but over the past few months Tim seemed to have been so occupied with his work that those sorts of dates had gone by the board. Sally stared unseeingly at the letter in front of her. Had she just been in love with the idea of being in love again and, encouraged by her parents' enthusiasm, persuaded herself that this was what she wanted in marriage?

Jack flicked a look at her sad face, her soft lips slightly drooping. 'A penny for them,' he murmured, putting his mug down on the table. 'Is it a very important letter there?' He lifted it gently out of her hands and flicked a glance at the letterhead. 'From the local health authority eh? Wow! That must be interesting. You seem to have read it about three times!'

Sally snatched back the letter crossly, startled out of her reverie. 'If you really want to know, it's about car parking…they want to use our car park, if you please, to put an enormous caravan in for some research project or other on cardiac problems.'

'So where will we park—and our patients?'

'You tell me! We're to have a meeting about it next week. Perhaps you can think of some arguments that will move them to change their minds.'

Jack laughed. 'I doubt it—health authorities are notoriously adamant about their proposals.'

He looked at her again doubtfully. 'You sure you're OK? You look very pale.'

Sally turned her head away, embarrassing tears stinging her eyes at his solicitous tone— very different from Tim, who hadn't seemed to notice what she'd looked like. She scrabbled surreptitiously for her handkerchief and dabbed at her eyes.

'I'm just a little tired, that's all,' she snapped.

He turned her face towards him then frowned, watching a solitary tear spill down her cheek. 'Hey…what's the matter? You look upset. Has something happened?'

His blue eyes were full of kind concern, gazing into hers, and he put his finger under her chin, tilting her face upwards. 'What is it, Sally?' he said gently. 'Can I help?'

For a second she was tempted to blurt out that her engagement wasn't the romantic idyll it should have been and offload her worry about the wedding—she remembered Jack had always been a good listener. Then she bit her lip. The concern in those eyes of his was a sham— he didn't care about her feelings and the last person she should ask advice from was Jack McLennan. for heaven's sake. He would probably say, 'I told you so—I knew you weren't suited!'

She pushed his hand away and sprang up from her chair. 'I'm OK!' she said irritably. 'Please leave me alone. There's nothing whatever the matter. I happened to have a bit of grit in my eye—that's all!' She walked to the other side of the room and turned back to him, eyes overly bright. 'We've got a practice meeting in a minute, Jack. Don't hassle me. I feel extremely well, actually.'

He looked at her quizzically. 'OK, fine...I believe you.'

There was the sound of voices outside the door and Joyce and Sharon came in, followed by Sula Janes, the practice nurse, and Bob Hedley, the practice manager.

Bob, a neat little man with owlish glasses, sat down at the end of the table and took some papers out of his briefcase.

'Right, everyone, please sit down,' he said briskly. 'Just a short meeting—I know surgery starts very soon so I won't prolong things. There are a few items on the agenda—the budget, of course, and the prescribing of drugs comes into that, and Sula's request for another practice nurse to help with the clinics.' He smiled around the table. 'But first a belated formal welcome to Jack McLennan. It's great that we've got someone to take over from Sally while she's on honeymoon...we'd have been in real trouble if we hadn't found him. And talking of honeymoons, how soon is it before you get married, Sally?'

Something seemed to catch in Sally's throat and her voice came out in a hoarse croak. 'Four weeks, actually.'

'Very exciting! I'm sure you can't wait. Never mind, time will fly by, I'm sure!'

'I suppose so,' said Sally with a weak smile.

She fought down the rising sense of panic she was beginning to feel every time she thought about the wedding—what was she going to do? If she was this unsure then obviously she should call the whole thing off immediately before the arrangements got any more complicated. She rested her throbbing head on her hand, trying to concentrate on the issues of BP tests on older patients, the number of appointments missed, and the difficulty in getting a cleaner to come in at the weekend.

'Right, I think that concludes almost everything,' said Bob at last, gathering up his papers. 'But before we go, and most importantly, the annual staff dinner needs to be organised, which, if you remember, we decided to hold now rather than at Christmas when everyone was so busy. Perhaps we could make it before Sally's wedding—a way of wishing her well before the big day!' He turned to Jack. 'We don't invite our nearest and dearest, only the people that work in the practice. Sally's final fling as a single girl, you might say!'

Everyone laughed and Sally managed to join in, although she felt slightly sick.

Sharon said excitedly, 'Can we go to that new Italian place on Hersa? It's a kind of disco and they do wonderful food…and there's plenty of ferries over there in the evening now.'

'A disco?' repeated Joyce, looking worried. 'Won't that be very loud?'

'Oh, no, Joyce,' Sharon assured her. 'And you know that dress I saw in that catalogue the other day I said would suit you? We'll send off for that—it would be perfect!'

'Sounds like fun,' Jack conceded.

'Oh, it is!' Sharon exclaimed. 'Do you like dancing, Dr McLennan?'

'Certainly I do. I used to dance a lot at one time...'

Perhaps he didn't mean to, but his amused blue eyes caught Sally's for a brief moment, enough to jog her memory and feel that flash of sadness and anger that unhappy memories sometimes brought...the final night they had been together after a wonderful evening at the hospital ball. Admittedly Jack had been quieter than usual and had arrived late after some hold-up, but he had been so tender, so sweet for the rest of the evening until...until he'd dumped her like a piece of trash in a junkyard, just when she'd thought they were at their happiest. And the excuse he'd given her for breaking up—his damned career, for heaven's sake! How dared he remind her of that?

And now, well, now it looked as if she'd made yet another mistake, getting entangled with a man she was sure didn't really love her, and whom she was beginning to realise perhaps she didn't love either.

Bob's brisk voice broke into her thoughts. 'Then I'll book at La Famiglia for next week, unless anyone has any other ideas? OK—meeting closed!'

The last thing Sally felt like doing was going to a disco and being cheerful. She needed peace and quiet for a while to reflect on her feelings for Tim—and his for her. Her mobile vibrating in her pocket reminded her that peace was going to be hard to find. She saw she had a text from her mother.

'Darling, just found an outfit for the wedding, but would like you to see it before I buy. Could you come over at the weekend?'

Sally groaned inwardly. She was beginning to feel as churned up as ingredients in a mixer.

She got up and walked slowly to the door. Jack watched her go out.

'See you later,' he said, thinking that she didn't look like a girl about to get married in a fairy-tale wedding to the love of her life. She looked unhappy and tired. More like someone who'd had bad news.

She nodded coldly at him, not in the mood to be friendly. He was just a colleague who would soon move on. He was nothing to do with her life now, although for some reason memories of their time together kept leaping into her mind, comparing the mad passion she'd once felt for him with her feelings now for Tim. And there was no contest, she suddenly realised—no weak-at-the-knees, heart-fluttering excitement when she saw Tim now, no searing response to his kisses, like there had been with Jack, when even a brush of hands was enough to send every erogenous zone in her body reeling.

She stood for a moment outside the door, then with sudden decision she marched to her room, took out her mobile and rang Tim's number. She wasn't going to leave a text—she had to speak to him now. The more she thought about it, the more she realised that they had been planning a marriage of convenience, something that had started as friendship and developed into a partnership that they'd both hoped would work.

When he answered he sounded surprised, slightly flustered. 'Sally? Something wrong? You don't usually phone me at this time of day.'

Not a very ebullient welcome, reflected Sally wryly. She decided to be blunt—why beat about the bush when time was running out? She took a deep breath, forcing herself to sound calm, not hysterical.

'I need to see you urgently, Tim. I have a horrible feeling that we're plunging into a marriage that isn't going to work. And I want you to be honest with me—have things been cooling off between us?'

There was a stunned silence then he said in a low voice, 'Sal, I can't discuss this now—I'm with a group of people.'

'I'm coming over to see you tonight, then. We need to have time alone to talk this over before our arrangements go any further.'

He hedged. 'If that's what you want…'

'It is, Tim,' she said firmly. 'I'll be with you at eight o'clock.'

She rang off and went to the window, pulling aside the blind and looking out at the sparkling sea and the peaceful mountains of Hersa beyond. She felt a certain amount of relief that she'd done something positive, mixed with sadness that it had come to this.

Tim's smart town flat looked over the river, expensively decorated in minimalist style with huge modern paintings on the wall. Sally sat on the enormous black leather sofa and looked around her, thinking how much it suited him, and how much her taste differed from his. He sat opposite her, leaning forward with a large drink in his hands, looking slightly ill at ease and, she noticed for the first time, without his usual brightness—just a rather weary expression.

'What do you want to say to me, Sally?' he asked, quite gently for him.

'I want to know what you feel about me,' she

said simply. Slowly she stirred the cup of coffee he'd given her. Her voice faltered a little, but she pressed on resolutely. 'You see, over the past few weeks we don't seem to have been...very close.'

He was silent for a few seconds, twirling his glass in his hands, then he looked up at her with misery in his eyes. 'I know...I'm so sorry, Sal,' he admitted at last. 'I thought we had a good thing going between us. I did really want to marry you, you know. I thought we'd make a good team.'

'So did I. Perhaps we were both lonely.' Sally looked at him sadly. 'But it's not going to work, is it? And I'm not blaming you, but I think there's someone else in your life now, isn't there?'

He rose from his seat and started to pace restlessly up and down in front of her. 'I didn't know how to tell you, and perhaps you guessed that Rita and I...well, we sort of got together over work. Actually,' he added with a grim smile, 'when she was helping to organise the wedding. We seemed to have the same ideas.'

'And you realised that we weren't so in tune with each other,' remarked Sally flatly.

'I couldn't bear to hurt you, and we'd got so far along the line with the wedding it seemed impossible to let you—and your parents—down. I really thought that the more we planned things, the more committed to each other we'd be.'

He wasn't a cruel man—he wanted to spare her feelings, unlike Jack, she thought bitterly. Jack hadn't seemed to care that he'd broken her heart. There'd been no finesse when he'd told her he no longer wanted to be involved with her—just a brutal severance.

Tim poured himself another whisky and walked over to Sally. 'I feel like a fool. It seemed such a good match, you and me, two lonely people. I never meant things to go wrong between us, believe me.'

She smiled up at him, suddenly feeling great relief that they were being honest with each other, able to say what they felt.

'I know you didn't, Tim. And I don't hold it against you. I guess we both got caught up in the excitement of getting married and didn't

allow ourselves time to really think about it.'
Sally sprang up and kissed him on the cheek.
'It's for the best, isn't it? I think we've both
realised that we're not meant for each other.'
She looked down at her finger and pulled off
the huge ring, putting it down on a little table,
its diamond winking and glittering in the evening sun from the window. 'You'd better have
this back. It's beautiful, but it deserves to go to
someone who really loves you.'

'Sally, I don't want it back.'

She put up her hand—funny how light and
unencumbered her finger felt! 'No, Tim.' She
picked her coat up from a chair. 'I'm not staying, but I won't say goodbye because I hope
we'll see each other again. We've had a lot of
fun together and I wish you all the best.'

Tim caught her hands. 'You're such a great
girl, Sally. You deserve someone better than
me anyway. Ask me to your wedding when you
meet the right fella!'

And that was all it took, thought Sally as
she drove back to Crannoch, a conversation of
about fifteen minutes to finish their engage-

ment. There was a sense of relief that she didn't have to pretend anymore to be excited about the wedding but also an empty kind of sadness that yet again she was on her own, and, most annoyingly, she could hear Jack's voice in her head saying smugly, 'I told you that Tim wasn't the man for you.'

CHAPTER SIX

'HAVE I many patients this afternoon?' Sally asked Joyce over the intercom at the end of a long morning surgery, during which a child had been sick on her floor and a patient had backed into her car, rendering it undrivable for the foreseeable future. It was one of the few mornings when being a GP had really tested her. Usually she loved the variety and unexpectedness of every case—not today!

Joyce's voice floated into the room. 'No. I kept it fairly free as you said you wanted to look through all the blood results and read your e-mails. There's only little Charlie Fleming and one or two recalls.'

That was a relief. There'd just be time to ring the garage about her car and walk to the hairdresser's in Crannoch at lunchtime to have her hair cut and blow-dried, for even though she'd decided not to go to the staff dinner that night, her hair still needed cutting. Somehow the thought of being cheerful and full of life with everyone enjoying themselves that evening seemed to be too much of an effort. Her finished relationship with Tim had been a relief, but she did feel a profound sadness that yet again she was alone. In some way she felt she'd failed both Tim and herself.

She put her chin in her hand and stared bleakly at Tim's photograph on the desk. No doubt about it. When it came to the opposite sex, she didn't have much luck! She'd grown used to having Tim around. However little they'd seen each other during the past few weeks, there'd been a certain comfort in knowing that someone cared for you, had your best interests at heart. Now there was no one.

Sadly she reached forward and tossed the photo into a drawer. She'd try not to waste months of her life mourning a lost relationship like she had done with Jack and she'd do her best not to hide herself away for the rest of her life just because she'd split up with her fiancé, but tonight it was too soon to go out and enjoy herself—the wound hadn't had a chance to heal. She would find some excuse to pull out of the evening…a bad headache, a fluey cold…

She hadn't yet told anyone that she and Tim were no longer engaged. The fact that she wasn't wearing her engagement ring wasn't unusual— sometimes she hadn't worn it to work anyway as it was so large and examining patients with it on had been a problem at times. Perhaps in a few days she would mention casually that the engagement was over when she'd got used to the idea herself and not make a big deal about it. She certainly wasn't going to make a point of disclosing it directly to Jack, because in some obscure way she felt that if she told him to his face, it was as if she was saying, 'So now I'm available again…' And that she was most certainly not—at least, not to Jack McLennan!

The worst part was informing her parents and assuring them that it really was for the best and it was a miracle that she and Tim had not drifted into marriage, despite feeling it was all wrong. To her surprise they had taken it relatively calmly, agreeing with her that an unhappy marriage was worse than no marriage at all. Her father had hugged her and said comfortingly in his kindly way, 'You'll meet Mr Right one of these days, pet, I feel it in my bones! But, to be honest, there's no one good enough for our Sal anyway!'

'Going anywhere nice?' Zac, the hairdresser, asked, blow-drying Sally's hair into a light fringe over her large grey eyes and flicking the sides into a bouncy curve round her neck.

She sighed. 'I was going out to dinner— La Famiglia on Hersa.'

'Oh, but you must go! You do look a little pale and tired—it would do you good. I love that place—wonderful food. And they have a little band there now that plays Italian music. So romantic!'

Sally smiled wanly. She couldn't see herself cuddling up to Bob Hedley, the practice manager, on the dance floor. And the only other male was Jack McLennan, and a romantic dance with him was quite out of the question, of course. No, romance was certainly not on the cards tonight.

'Voilà!' exclaimed Zac, narrowing his eyes as he looked at Sally's face in the mirror. 'You look exquisite! Go out and enjoy yourself!'

If only it was that easy—but you couldn't just flick a switch and go from sad to happy, could you?

There was no doubt about it—little Charlie Fleming had measles! His face was flushed, his eyes heavy and listless, and there was a blotchy rash on his neck, which had spread like a raised stain over his chest.

'Are you absolutely sure, Dr Lawson?' Mrs Fleming looked tired and anxious—she had two other children as well as Charlie.

Sally switched on her torch. 'Open your mouth, sweetheart—let me have a peep inside…' She directed it to illuminate the back of Charlie's throat. 'As sure as I can be. There's some white spots around the skin inside his mouth—we call them Koplik's spots and that's a good indicator, given all his other symptoms.' She flicked through the little boy's notes on the screen. 'Take him home and give him plenty of fluids. Call us if he gets worse, or sounds chesty, but hopefully he'll feel better in a few days.'

Sally had an ominous feeling that this wouldn't be the only case that would show up in the area. Measles were highly contagious and Charlie went to a local nursery school. She made a note to contact Charlie's school and the health protection agency. If there was going to be an epidemic they needed to be informed and a formal notification certificate completed so that the illness could be tracked for local and national trends. Something else to be crammed into the already crowded schedule of a busy practice.

God, she felt tired! Sally pressed her fingers to her eyes. The emotions of the past few days had really taken it out of her. Grimly she reflected that what she needed was a holiday—somewhere remote and beautiful with no patients, but not alone. She didn't feel like going off somewhere by herself when she should have been on honeymoon. Then she bit her lip, irritated by her maudlin manner—it was no good feeling sorry for herself. She sat up, briskly determined to make a start on the backlog of e-mails giving patients' blood results before she went home to a hot bath and a comforting glass of wine. As she scrolled down the e-mails there was a knock on the door and Jack appeared, looking the opposite of how she felt, Sally observed wryly. He exuded energy and looked tanned and cheerful.

'Just wanted to know if I could give you a lift tonight. I hear someone's put your car out of action. Bob's taking the others across on the car ferry, but we can't all get into his car.'

Sally shook her head. 'Thanks—but no thanks. I…I'm afraid I've decided not to go tonight.'

Jack raised an eyebrow in surprise. 'Not go? Aren't you feeling too good?' Then he added rather smugly, 'I told you I thought you looked off-colour the other day.'

'I'm just a little overtired, I suppose,' said Sally irritably.

'It might do you good…perk you up a little and take your mind off all the arrangements you've been making.'

'I really don't want…' she began firmly.

Jack looked at her rather reproachfully. 'Don't you think you ought to come if you possibly can? Everyone wants to give you a good send-off for the wedding.'

Sally slumped at the desk and put her head in her hands. 'Oh, God, how awful!'

'Sally?' Jack walked towards the desk and put a hand on her shoulder, looking down at her in concern. 'Is something wrong? Is it Tim?'

She looked up at Jack sharply. 'What do you mean…Tim?'

Jack shrugged. 'Well, is he jealous or something? Doesn't want you to go out this evening without him?'

She took a deep breath and said in a prim little voice, 'Don't be totally ridiculous, Jack. It's nothing to do with Tim. I'm my own woman—I can do what I like. It's just that…'

He grinned. 'Being engaged means you can't go out by yourself perhaps?'

Sally flushed angrily. 'I've just told you, Tim doesn't rule my life.'

He put up a hand as if defending himself. 'Hey! I'm only joking, you know!'

Sally closed her eyes for a second and then sighed. 'Sorry—slight sense of humour bypass there I'm afraid.' She paused, fiddling with a pencil then blurted out recklessly, 'The thing is, Tim and I aren't engaged anymore.'

Jack's eyes widened and he looked at her in amazement. 'You and he broke up…?'

'We…we decided we weren't suited to each other—we're not engaged anymore, but it's all been very amicable.' Her voice was defiant. 'And don't say you told me it wouldn't work out!'

There was a shocked silence, then Jack commented drily, 'I wouldn't dream of it.' He looked at her searchingly. 'So the wedding's off. No regrets?'

'It was the right thing to do so, no, I've no regrets. But of course I feel sad…and I really don't think I can cope with being all merry and bright tonight.'

Jack sat at the edge of the desk. 'Have you told anyone else?'

'Only my parents. I'm still coming to terms with it. I'll tell everyone in a day or two…it still feels pretty raw.'

Jack nodded. 'I guess so…' He leaned forward slightly, his eyes looking into hers persuasively. 'However, you're not the type to sit moping at home, are you? And after all you'd be letting everyone down—you're the senior doctor here at the moment.'

Those eyes of his were slightly disconcerting somehow, the way they held hers so compellingly, as if expecting more of her than to just give in and spend the evening by herself. He had always been very persuasive… She sighed. Perhaps Jack was right and it was feeble not to make the effort.

'I'll think about it,' she said guardedly.

Jack got up and grinned. 'My advice would be to come out and let your hair down a bit—have a little fun. You might be surprised how easy it is! I'll pick you up at seven, unless you tell me not to!'

As he walked down the corridor to his room, a curious mixture of elation and sadness flickered through him. He was hardly able to believe the news Sally had just given him—she and Tim were no longer getting married! He walked up and down his room restlessly, trying to digest the fact that now Sally was free—free to go out with anyone if she wanted. Even him, he thought wistfully. What a pity that he was as far away from commitment as ever he had been… and yet how tempting it would be to test the ground, to grab this second chance of happiness.

Still restless, he went to the window, pulled back the blind and stared unseeingly out at the view. He supposed he wasn't really surprised that Sally and Tim hadn't stayed the course—somehow they hadn't seemed like twin souls to him, and their relationship seemed to have been conducted almost at a distance. Jack's thoughts went back to when he and Sally had fallen in love. They had hardly been able to have a day apart, longing to spend every moment together, feverish in their desire to be close to each other. And when they'd been together, they hadn't been able to keep their hands of each other—

how the sparks had flown! His lips curved in a sad smile of remembrance.

And now? Oh, he loved Sally as much as he ever had, but he could never risk hurting her again. If she knew what had happened in his family, how tainted they all were by his father's actions, what would her reaction be? Her feelings towards him now were, at best, very negative. If she was aware of the true reason that had driven him away from her, how would she view him then, a traitor who'd betrayed his family, split them apart?

Jack ran a distracted hand through his thick hair, leaving it tousled and rather wild. The truth was, of course, that in her eyes he'd betrayed her years ago when he'd left her so abruptly.

Sally flicked a look at her watch and groaned inwardly. Just when she'd thought she'd finished for the day Sharon had informed her that there was a girl who needed to see a doctor urgently, adding in a voice full of suppressed excitement that she was a well-known film star who'd been making a film nearby.

At the moment Sally's brain felt like cotton wool after her conversation with Jack. Why the hell had she been stupid enough to reveal to him that she and Tim were finished? He was the last person she'd wanted to tell. He wasn't part of her life anymore, and she certainly hadn't meant to blurt out what had happened. She hated the thought that she would appear needy and vulnerable to Jack! What she desperately wanted was peace and quiet to reflect on her new situation and not a night out. She bit her lip in frustration and tried to clear her head to deal with a spoilt celebrity who probably had some minor affliction that couldn't wait until the morning!

Sharon had written the patient's name down on a piece of paper: 'Careena Fairfax'. Sally had seen her on television and in the papers at various first nights—a glamorous young woman. She'd also seen the huge parade of mobile homes and lorries carrying filming equipment and all the personnel needed for a film going inland towards the hills outside Crannoch.

Careena Fairfax entered, reed slim in tight

blue jeans, thick blonde hair pulled back in a bunch behind her head and large violet eyes that were her trade mark in a heart-shaped face. She was even more breathtakingly beautiful in the flesh than on the screen, but across her cheek was a vivid red line, and the skin had bubbled into tiny blisters.

'It's kind of you to see me so promptly, Doctor,' Careena said in a deep, husky voice. She sank down on the chair and looked mournfully at Sally. 'It's my hands—they've become agonisingly painful this afternoon. And now my cheek seems to have come up with this horrible weal. I don't know how I'll get on tomorrow— we're doing a really important scene and this isn't going to look too good on camera.'

'Let me see. Put your hands on the desk.' Sally peered at the palms and drew in her breath sharply. 'Goodness, that does look very painful. You've got blisters forming on the skin.'

She turned on the angled lamp on her desk and positioned it over the affected skin. The area was red, raw and swollen, and blisters were forming almost as she looked, as was the line of red skin across Careena's face. Sally changed her mind about famous people wanting special attention—the poor woman must be really suffering.

'It almost looks as though you've burnt yourself,' she said at last, frowning in puzzlement. 'Are you allergic to anything?'

'No, I don't think so… Why, do you think I've had a reaction to something?'

'It looks like it. Just where are you filming?'

'In that little valley about a mile up the road, by the river.' Careena made a face. 'It looks idyllic, but when you've done about twenty-five takes of a scene it begins to lose its charm.'

'Then I'm guessing that you've got an allergy to something in the vegetation there,' said Sally, reaching for her prescription pad. 'I'm going to give you some anti-histamines, but I think you need a dressing on those hands and your face—they mustn't get infected.'

Careena looked at her anxiously. 'Do you think they can stop it being so painful? I've got to be on location tomorrow. But the worst thing is my face—it looks horrible. The producer will go mad if the scene has to be postponed.'

Sally shook her head in bewilderment. 'Do you mind if I ask a colleague of mine to come in? He might possibly have an idea what caused it.' She pressed the intercom connecting her to the receptionists. 'Is Dr McLennan with a patient, Jean? If he's available, would you ask him to come in here and give his opinion on something?'

A few seconds later Jack appeared: Careena's worried face relaxed slightly as she looked appreciatively at his handsome face—a hero doctor who might feature in one of her films, Sally thought wryly. He had the kind of reliable manner and looks that seemed to dispel anxiety as he strode confidently into the room. She grimaced to herself. Women fell so easily for a man like Jack—just as she had once upon a time.

'You wanted me?' he enquired.

Sally dismissed her thoughts and introduced her patient briskly. 'This is Miss Fairfax.'

'I think I recognise you.' Jack smiled. 'You're filming up in the glen, aren't you?'

'Yes, but I don't know for how long,' sighed the blonde. 'And call me Careena.'

Sally took Careena's arm and held it palm upwards to Jack. 'I wondered if you'd ever come across a condition like this on the hands and face. She's been down by the river all afternoon, and I'm sure it's an allergy of some kind—but what?'

Jack looked at the affected skin closely, turning Careena's face gently to one side and inspecting the livid mark on her cheek. Then he nodded rather grimly. 'I haven't seen this reaction for a long time, but I think I have a good idea why you've formed these blisters. You tell me you've been filming by the river—my guess is that you've been in contact with something called giant hogweed. Did you notice tall plants with huge flowerheads? Could be fifteen feet high. They look rather like enormous cow parsley plants?'

Careena nodded. 'There were masses of them by the river bank. I pulled them aside when

I had to run through the vegetation doing all those takes this morning. Surely just touching them couldn't give me all these blisters?'

'I'm afraid it's entirely possible. Where I've been living in Australia they've been declared a noxious weed,' said Jack. 'You must go to Casualty—these lesions are true burns and need to be treated as such.'

Sally nodded. 'And I think we'd better inform the film unit what they're exposing themselves to or else the whole cast may be affected.'

'It looks like they might have to postpone filming, then…' Careena's voice trailed off and she looked anguished. 'If the film goes over budget they may not finish it—this was going to be my big breakthrough for Hollywood!'

She went out of the room and on to Casualty with the note Jack had given them. Sally could see Sharon hovering by the door, waiting to catch a glimpse of the star, which would make her day!

'What kind of poison is it?' Sally asked Jack as she shut down her computer preparatory to going home.

'It's a clear sap that's found in the stem and stem hairs—it sensitises the skin to ultraviolet radiation for some time.'

'Oh, dear…poor Careena. I've seen those plants by the river, but I'd no idea they were so dangerous.' She paused for a second and then said briefly, 'Thanks for sorting it out.'

'No problem. I take it I'm still picking you up tonight?'

Sally hesitated. She wasn't about to get too friendly with Jack just because he'd managed to diagnose what had caused Careena's allergy. She really wanted to be completely independent now. And, anyway, she didn't want to be beholden to Jack in any way—or to any man.

'It's all right, thanks,' she said lightly. 'It's not far to walk to the quayside.'

'Oh, come on.' He grinned, his eyes dancing as if he knew very well she was trying to keep her distance. 'The ferry's at the other end of town…and just think of staggering there in high heels!'

That was true. There was also the fact that La

Famiglia was up in the hills beyond the ferry on Hersa and quite a hike.

'I'll be ready at seven, then,' she said coolly. 'Thanks for the offer. I'd better get going now. Things to do and I could do with a brisk walk home to clear my head before we go out.'

Sally riffled through the things in her wardrobe—many of the things she wore when going out with Tim looked rather grand and formal because he liked to go to all the important big functions in Glasgow. What on earth was she going to wear tonight? And why should it matter anyway as long as she looked presentable? And yet she wanted to look her best for…well, her own sense of pride, she supposed. Or, a small voice whispered in her head, was it because she wanted to show Jack that after six years she could still look pretty good? And that even if he had been right in his assumption that Tim hadn't been the man for her, she could hold her head up high and dress for herself and not just to please a man.

She needed something simple and yet elegant,

but not an outfit that had to make a huge state-ment. With a wry smile she took down from a hanger a silk peach-coloured sheath dress that she'd bought a few weeks ago for her honey-moon. She may as well wear it now as she prob-ably wouldn't get many occasions to wear it in the future.

She slipped it on and looked critically at her-self in the mirror. Was it a bit too revealing for the practice dinner? It certainly fitted her well, emphasising the soft swell of her breasts and clinging provocatively around her curves, but it wasn't fussy and it was cool and comfortable for a warm late May evening. She found a chain with an amber pendant and put it round her neck, where it nestled at the base of her throat, and sprayed some perfume lightly over herself. Then, slipping the high heels on she'd bought with the dress, she gave a final glance at herself in the mirror.

The front doorbell rang and she ran down-stairs, and unexpectedly, because going out was the last thing she wanted to do, a little ripple of excitement fluttered through her. It was about time that she started to enjoy herself again. She saw Jack's tall figure through the glass in the door and thought wistfully back to how she used to run to meet him for a date, the whole evening before them, her heart racing in anticipation. And now it would be the first time for six years that they'd been out together socially. She came to a halt just before the door and took a deep breath. She and Jack weren't an item anymore—it was over and done with, and had been for many years. She mustn't forget that.

She opened the door and the light from the porch illuminated her figure. Jack looked at her silently for a moment, his eyes darkening as they swept over her soft contours and took in the creaminess of her skin against the soft peach colour of the dress. He smiled that familiar sweet smile, one side of his mouth quirking slightly, and gave a low whistle.

'You look beautiful,' he murmured. He stepped aside and indicated his car. 'Your carriage awaits, ma'am.'

She flicked a look at him as they walked down the garden path towards the car, one of his long strides taking two of hers. He wore an open-necked shirt, a navy jacket and his long legs were encased in beige chinos—casual suited him. Almost as a reflex action, force of habit from the old days, she nearly put her hand out to take his—just in time, she moved a step further away.

The car drove onto the little ferry and they got out to lean together over the rails and watch the creamy wake of the boat as they went over the Hersa Sound. It was a beautiful evening, the pale blue sky tinged with pink as the sun touched the top of the hills of Hersa, and the air was cool and sweet.

'Look at that,' whispered Jack suddenly, pointing towards the open sea.

'Where? What is it?'

He moved nearer to Sally, putting an arm round her shoulder and turning her towards the place he wanted her to look.

'See that slight disturbance in the water over there? Watch it closely!'

For a second the unexpectedness of his arm round her made her jump, and she tensed as every nerve became conscious of the warmth of his body next to hers. Then she forgot about him for a few minutes, as out of the turbulence in the sea a line of torpedo-shaped bodies suddenly launched themselves out of the water, spinning in the air, arcing in a graceful curve before plunging back and following the boat in graceful harmony, like synchronised swimmers.

Sally watched entranced and turned to smile in delight at him. 'A pod of dolphins,' she breathed. 'I don't think I've seen any as near as this…what a thrill! It's marvellous, isn't it?'

They both laughed together at the wonderful creatures and Sally tilted her head back to watch them soaring effortlessly out of the sea so close to them. Jack watched her profile hungrily, the breeze blowing her dress against her curvaceous body, her hair whipping across her face. He knew she held a deep distrust of him still, although occasionally he felt there was something of the old rapport between them. Then unexpectedly during the little interlude they'd just experienced it had been almost like it had been in the past—laughing in happiness together over something they enjoyed. He sighed and dropped his arm from round her shoulder—he supposed it would be something if she could even bring herself to feel he was a friend.

CHAPTER SEVEN

LA FAMIGLIA was a cheerful little restaurant run by an Italian couple. There were red-and-white checked tablecloths on the table, and large candles stuck in glass holders threw a soft but pleasantly warm light over the room. On the walls were huge photographs of Venice, Rome and Milan and a little band played soft Italian music in the background.

Seeing the dolphins seemed to have got the evening off to a wonderful start, and Sally forgot that she hadn't been looking forward to coming out at all. She began to relax and enjoyed the light-hearted banter between Sharon, Bob and Sula. She felt a new sense of freedom, no longer worrying about her relationship with Tim, no plans to make—just a glorious feeling of liberation.

Bob had ordered wine and poured some out

for everyone, even Joyce who daringly agreed to have a small glass. The only person who refused and ordered a tonic water was Jack. Sally was surprised—she could remember when she'd gone out with him that he'd loved a beer. During the meal Bob stood up, pushing back his chair and clearing his throat.

'I think we ought to drink—' he began.

A feeling of acute embarrassment flooded over Sally. She was sure he was about to toast her forthcoming wedding and she didn't feel like confessing that it was all off—that would surely put a dampener on the party. She could only hope they hadn't brought a present with them. Hearing the beat of the little band quickening, she leaned forward, intending to beg Sharon and Sula to get up an dance with her, but before she could ask them, Jack was standing in front of her and had taken her hand, pulling her up to dance with him. He started by spinning her giddily round the floor, and everyone at the table laughed and clapped.

'I thought it might be appropriate to cause a

slight diversion there,' he murmured into her ear, before twirling her again.

'Thank you,' whispered Sally. 'It could have been awkward.'

He squeezed her hand. 'You're bearing up well. I told you it wouldn't be too bad!'

He was right, Sally thought. It was amazing how uninhibited a glass or two of wine could make you feel, although she was aware that her hair was flying about wildly and her dress was a little too decolleté for this kind of activity—but, then, what did it matter? It was the first time for ages that she'd felt carefree, unshackled by the thought of her impending wedding. As Jack spun her round she caught the amused expression on his face, his eyes dancing with laughter as she flung herself into the dance. So what? she thought. The fact was, she was enjoying herself—and it was doing her good!

The music stopped for a while and the dancers in the party came off the floor and breathlessly flung themselves into their chairs.

Joyce had ended up dancing with Sharon and Sula and fanned her face with a napkin. 'I haven't taken so much exercise in years,' she declared as she flopped down. 'My feet will never be the same, thanks to you girls!'

Bob looked at his watch. 'I'm sorry, everyone,' he said. 'I've booked us on the ten-thirty ferry as I've got some way to drive back, so I think I'd better take my passengers now. I take it you're on the next one?' he asked Jack.

Jack nodded. 'There was only room on the last one of the evening, and that doesn't go for about an hour. Don't worry though, Sally and I can use the time to catch up on some practice matters anyway.'

'Sounds a riveting way to end the evening.' Sharon giggled. 'What a shame you have to wait for the next ferry.'

'Well everything's paid for,' said Bob. 'Have fun!'

The others collected their coats and after much laughter, shouted their goodbyes and disappeared to get into Bob's car and catch the ferry back to the mainland. Sally and Jack were left sitting at the table together. Sally felt a little light-headed and leaned back against the wall, thinking that perhaps she shouldn't have had quite so much wine, but after the emotional roller-coaster she'd been on, it had done her a world of good.

She watched Jack sipping his tonic water. 'You're being very careful,' she remarked archly. 'You're allowed a beer, you know.'

'This does me fine,' he said dismissively. He grinned at her. 'You can do the drinking.'

'Oops…are you telling me I've had too much?'

'Not at all. I'm glad you're enjoying yourself.'

Sally watched the dancers as the band had started up again, this time it was a slow, languid beat. She was unaware of Jack's scrutiny as he looked at her shining blonde bob, her pert profile and her soft creamy skin, set off by the colour of the silky peach dress. How totally sexy and desirable she looked! How very unwise it would be to dance with her to this slow tune now the rest of the party had gone and there were just the two of them left together. He stood up and put out his hand, pulling her to her feet again.

'What about a dance, Sally?' he murmured. 'For old times' sake?'

For old times' sake? Sally wasn't prepared for the jolt of nostalgia that had flickered through her when he'd said those words. They'd had such good times together all those years ago—such very sweet moments absorbed in each other, aware only of the attraction between them. Was it really safe to think back to those times when it seemed her future with Jack had been safely mapped out before her?

'I thought you wanted to discuss practice business,' she protested, hanging back.

'We'll do that on the dance floor...'

She frowned up at him, the wine and the pleasure of the evening making her feel slightly woozy but still cautious enough to be wary of close physical contact with Jack again. 'I...I don't know if I should dance with you, Jack.'

'Why not? Tell me one good reason. You're a free spirit now, remember?'

His startling blue eyes danced humorously across at her and he pushed his thick auburn hair back from his forehead. God, he was so attractive—no wonder she'd fallen for him all those years ago. Then, despite her reservations about this man, she felt a shiver of raw desire through her body and knew that all evening— ever since he'd put his arm round her shoulder on the ferry in fact—she had been intensely aware of him, unable to forget the way they used to kiss—and how great that had been.

Her cheeks reddened, knowing that, far from not wanting to dance with Jack, she couldn't wait for him to put his arms round her and sway to the music! How odd was that—to want to dance with a rat who'd betrayed her, lied to her?

Perhaps it was a reaction to the loneliness of a broken engagement, perhaps it was a sudden sweet memory of how it had once been when they'd danced together, or probably because she'd had too much to drink! Well, she wasn't going to give into her basic instincts of sexual attraction to him that easily!

Jack noticed her reticence and pulled her fiercely towards him and onto the dance floor. 'You don't have any excuses not to dance with me,' he murmured.

And it was true, of course, but now Tim was no longer around, perhaps Jack thought she was available again, free to have a bit of fun with, and then, when it came time to leave the practice, to disappear into thin air again, reflected Sally cynically. Somehow she couldn't face doing a rerun of that scenario, because she was beginning to realise that it would be so, so easy to fall for Jack again—and she certainly wasn't going to do that! She'd learned her lesson big time.

His body was hard and muscular against hers. He was so close to her that she could feel the thud of his heartbeat as he held her tightly to his chest, felt the movement of his hips against hers… The room was lit mainly by candlelight and there was a dreamy atmosphere on the dance floor, heightened by the sweet voice of the singer. Jack bent his face down and pressed his cheek against hers so that she could feel the light evening stubble against her skin and smell the slight hint of cologne on his neck. And as they swayed, closely locked to each other, she realised that what she had felt for Tim was nothing compared to the fizzing, raw sexual attraction for Jack that still held her even now, still overwhelmed her. And it seemed entirely natural that his mouth should brush against hers lightly but enough to make her lips tingle. They almost ceased to dance, just swaying back and forth together, their bodies locked together.

At the back of her mind she heard a little voice whisper, *This is dangerous, Sally. Be very, very careful. This man deluded you cruelly once upon a time.* She pushed that voice away firmly.

Then the music came to a stop, the lights came up slowly and they stood still, Jack's arms around her, her head on his chest, her eyes closed.

Jack looked down at Sally with an unreadable expression on his face. What the hell was he doing, torturing himself, dancing so close to Sally, even kissing her? Was he completely mad? When Sally had told him that she and Tim had split up he'd felt a momentary dizzy joy that she was free once more—then that hollow feeling of despair had returned when he'd realised that nothing had changed really. He could never commit to anyone.

He dropped his hands to her waist and pressed his lips to her forehead, almost in despair. 'Oh, Sally,' he said huskily. 'It's been so long…so long since I've held you like this…'

Sally's eyes flew open and she gazed up at him, startled out of her dream-like state. She stepped back from him hastily, suddenly filled with embarrassment. Why the hell had she agreed to dance with him? Why had she gone so willingly onto the dance floor into Jack's arms and allowed him to hold her so closely, even to kiss her, albeit very chastely? The answer was simple. That demon of burning sexual desire had blotted out how much she disliked, dis-trusted the man, the last person in the world that she should have been close to. It had been a mad little interlude which she would have to put out of her mind.

'Funny,' she said with a shaky little laugh. 'I forgot where we were for a minute…'

'So did I,' murmured Jack, putting his hand behind her waist and guiding her back to the table. 'I thought we were back at St Mary's at the end-of-year ball six years ago, dancing the night away. It had been such a good evening...' His voice trailed off as if he'd suddenly remembered how the evening had ended.

She whirled round to him then, suddenly jolted by his words into recalling that evening and all the shattered dreams it had brought. The contrast between how she felt a moment ago in his arms and the reminder of the unspeakable hurt Jack had caused her at the end of the hospital ball was stark and cruel. She gave a little gasp of fury and like a dam that had burst its walls the pent-up anger she'd had simmering away inside her boiled over, and words she hadn't been able to say to him over the years spilled out in a torrent of fury.

'I don't know how you can mention that evening,' she said in a low, furious voice. 'You treated me as casually as someone you'd known for a week rather than a year, throwing me aside like a piece of rubbish.'

He looked totally taken aback at her sudden vehemence. 'But, Sally, it was six years ago.

Can't you forgive me after all this time? A lot of water's gone under the bridge since then… and I had my reasons.' He searched her face frowningly, his own face pale in the dim light.

Her grey eyes sparked angrily across at him. 'You told me a pack of lies—said that you loved me and wanted to be with me for ever. Then a few weeks later you came up with this incredible excuse to get rid of me—that you wanted to concentrate on your career. I'd have thought more of you if you'd told me face to face that you no longer fancied me!'

He shook his head and said vehemently, 'Of course I fancied you. I loved you to distraction.' His voice dropped. 'But I knew that we had to finish that night. Something happened, something that meant I couldn't commit to you after all. I kept putting it off until the dance ended because it was such a magical evening…and I knew I would lose you for ever. Believe me, I could hardly bear to do it. It…it tore me apart.'

'Really?' Sally's voice was icy. 'Then why did you go out with me at all?'

'Because I was crazy for you, Sally.' He was

silent for a second then said sadly, 'But circumstances changed…I realised I couldn't become permanently involved, that was all.'

'That was all?' She looked at him incredulously. 'You put me through months of hell because it wasn't quite the right time to commit to me, is that it? Your damn career came before me—I would be a hindrance to your terrific progress up the ladder of success, I suppose.'

'I thought it would be unfair to you.'

'What rubbish! It was an insult. And if you still loved me to distraction, why did you never write to me? You just disappeared off the radar. I tell you something, it'll take more than a few minutes on the dance floor to wipe out what you did to me that evening, Jack.'

Her voice was low and furious, painful memories making the words spill out aggressively, trying to wound him. People started to look at them, poised like two boxers about to spar with each other. For some stupid reason Sally felt tears pricking her eyes as the angst of all those years ago poured out of her. She moved back to their table, and sat down abruptly, staring straight ahead of her. Jack sat down beside her and took her hand.

'I can never repair the damage I did to you, Sally,' he said softly. 'I'm so, so sorry.'

She snatched her hand away, impatiently brushing a tear away from her eye at his gentle words. 'Sorry?' she said scornfully. 'I'd be out of my mind to believe a word you said again. You're nothing but a…a…' She searched in frustration for a word bad enough to describe him.

A ghost of a smile flickered across his face. 'A rat?' he supplied with a glimmer of the humour she knew so well. 'OK, OK—I get the point, and of course you're right. I behaved in a hellish way towards you.' He ran his hand distractedly through his hair so that it stood up in little tufts round his head, and he looked so contrite and rather comical that Sally almost felt sorry for him—almost, but not quite.

'Then why did you do it, Jack?' She looked at him fiercely, as if trying to read his mind. 'I'm confused. We were so happy together…if you really loved me, the timing shouldn't have mattered at all. Tell me the truth.'

Jack closed his eyes for a second. If he had told Sally the truth that night she would have dismissed his fears, told him she didn't care what his parents did, or the social stigma attached to his family, assured him that just because his father had been an alcoholic, it didn't mean he would be one too. But he couldn't take the risk. He knew how the finger pointing and the whispering campaign would start, and how it could destroy lives.

He twirled an empty glass, staring unseeingly across the room as couples danced, and he relived the horror of living with a parent who was an alcoholic and the breakdown of family life it caused. He remembered the agony his mother had gone through, trying to keep the worst of his father's excesses from her children, bundling them into a bedroom while his father had raged in the room below. He remembered hearing him screaming at her, hitting her in a drunken stupor. He remembered putting his hands over his little brother's ears, trying to shield him from the terror they'd both felt. His father had inherited his own father's love of drink—it could be that he'd passed this terrible legacy down to Jack as well.

'You have to believe me,' he said harshly, his face brooding and strangely set. 'I'm just not marriage material.'

Sally leapt up angrily, two bright spots of colour on her cheeks, her fists clenched by her sides. 'That's just not good enough, Jack,' she spat out. 'I've listened to these cryptic excuses for long enough. Just what is it that makes you so different from anyone else? There's something you're not telling me.' She reached down to grab her handbag and pulled the pashmina she'd worn over her dress from the back of a chair. 'I'm leaving. I'd rather walk to the ferry than wait here with you. What the hell are you afraid of that you can't tell me the truth?'

He took one stride towards her and held her arm in a vice-like grip. 'OK, OK,' he said harshly. 'You want the unvarnished truth…I'll tell you.' His blue eyes blazed at her in the semi-darkness. 'Perhaps it doesn't matter anyway now that I realise you've kept up a simmering hatred for me all these years.'

Did she hate him? The candlelight from the table lit up his strong, good-looking face—the face that had featured in so many of her dreams for so long after he'd left her. Surely he could understand just what he'd done to her, how he'd taken away her self-esteem and shattered her judgement? But, despite that, the answer was, no, of course she didn't hate him. Her feelings towards him were hard to define but it was definitely not hate…

'I just wish you hadn't told me you loved me so much before dropping such a bombshell on me,' she said bitterly.

He pulled her down in a chair beside him again. 'You're right. I shouldn't have done that.' He was silent for a moment then gave a twisted smile. 'The fact is I didn't want you to become embroiled with a dysfunctional family like mine—and the terrible incident that brought it all to a head.'

'What on earth do you mean?'

Jack swirled the mineral water round in his

glass for a second, watching the bubbles rise to the surface. Then, looking directly at her, he said in a low, harsh voice, 'Three days before I was due back at the hospital on the day of the ball, my father killed someone. He knocked a girl off her bike when he was driving and had been drinking heavily. The girl was killed as she landed on the bonnet of the car. I was the only witness, the only one to see him drive away at speed from the scene of the accident like a rat from a sinking ship.'

The staccato phrases, the bald way they'd been presented, hung in the air—horrifying, unimaginable. In the background the jaunty music sounded ill matched to the terrible story Jack had told her, and the laughter and chatter of the people in the restaurant at odds to the atmosphere in the alcove.

Sally took a deep breath, stunned to silence as she thought back to the night of the hospital ball. Jack had had some days off and been to see his parents but had been returning that afternoon. She'd received a text about an hour before he was due to pick her up. 'Running late. Take taxi to dance. See you there, love J.'

She remembered when he'd arrived he'd looked incredibly tired, grey and spent, but she'd put it down to the long drive back from his parents'. And all that evening he had been quiet, unlike his usual ebullient self, an odd expression of abstraction on his face. If only she had known what had really happened…

'How…how terrible. What an awful thing to have witnessed. But why couldn't you have told me?' she said in anguish. 'I'd have understood. It wasn't your fault.'

'I knew you would have said it didn't matter, that it shouldn't come between us.' Jack's face was stony. 'But my whole family was ripped apart by that tragedy—and I couldn't risk dragging you into it and ruining your life too. When my father married my mother, her life and her children's lives were all coloured by his behaviour…he was a drunken bully and a murderer. He killed that girl because he was arrogant—he never believed that drink affected him. He made our family life a misery.'

Sally said firmly, 'But you rose above that, Jack. You became a doctor, made your own life. I can't believe that you would finish things between us—our chance of happiness—because of what your father did.'

'You have to believe it,' Jack said harshly. 'You have no idea, with your happy family life, your idyllic childhood, what living with a drunken, bullying father is like. The consequences that followed that crash tainted us for ever—affected my life, my thinking.'

That was true, reflected Sally. Jack's past had been very different from hers—he'd had to cope with so much.

'What…what happened to your father?' asked Sally, embarrassed to ask but feeling she had to know the whole story.

'He went to jail—and my mother never spoke to me again…'

'But why not?' Sally searched his grim face in bewilderment. 'Why should she punish you?'

'Because I told the police—I shopped him. In her eyes I was a traitor—I broke up the family.' A bitter smile touched his lips. 'My father bullied her, abused her, but she still loved him more than she did me—made excuses for him.'

Sally shook her head wordlessly, horrified at the picture Jack had painted.

'Now can you see why I couldn't commit to you?' he said harshly. 'I brought too much baggage with me Sally. I come from a long line of alcoholics. Who's to say I wouldn't end up that way too? I wouldn't wish what happened to our family on anyone.'

'But that's only speculation. You can't help your background,' Sally cried.

'You say that now,' Jack said with a faint smile. 'When your family heard about my illustrious parents they might have held different views.' He shrugged dismissively. 'Anyway… it's of small consequence now because we're not together. In fact, you've just told me in no uncertain terms that you've harboured a distinct dislike of me for a long time.' There was a hint of wistfulness in his expression. 'I thought you might have got over me finishing our relationship by now.'

I thought I'd got over you too, thought I hated

you, but I was wrong, Sally reflected bleakly, distractedly twisting a napkin with her hands. And if she was honest, far from hating him, didn't every nerve in her body react when he was close—attracted like iron filings to a magnet, much more so than she'd ever felt for Tim? And because she now knew the terrible reason behind his rejection of her, it would be the easiest thing in the world to fall for this man again.

Jack sat down on the edge of a chair and turned towards Sally. 'When I came back a few weeks ago, I realised you disliked me—not surprising, but I'd hoped that you'd learn to tolerate me. After all, you were engaged and had made a new life for yourself.' He paused for a second, looking at her steadily. 'I have to admit that I find it rather hard to work with someone who so patently isn't over the moon about working with me.' He put his hands up to silence her as she opened her mouth in protest. 'Listening to you now has shown me only too clearly that I was wrong to assume that you could forgive me. Obviously you'd prefer to work with someone who didn't remind you of an unhappy time in your life.' He looked at her sadly and added quietly, 'And that's why I think it would be best if I moved on.'

Sally looked at him stunned, totally taken aback. 'Moved on? B-but you can't d-do that...' she stammered. 'You...you said you'd work here until Jean came back from New Zealand...'

He shrugged. 'I don't want to let you down but, from what you just said, you've never forgotten the hurt I caused you. The best solution is for me to leave, and after all, you won't need time off for a honeymoon now. I think it's better for both of us that we don't work together anymore.'

CHAPTER EIGHT

THERE was total silence between them and Sally stared at Jack in disbelief, her heart lurching uncomfortably against her ribs. Work without him? She bit her lip. She didn't want him to go—who would she get at such short notice? He was a good doctor, the patients had taken to him in a big way and, dammit, she would miss him…quite a lot, in fact. Suddenly the realisation hit her that she couldn't go all her life hating Jack for what he'd done to her.

A few minutes ago she'd exploded with bitter recriminations, but now it was as if a boil had been lanced. The poison had gone. In fact, to her surprise, when she thought about it, 'dislike' was the wrong word for what she felt for Jack. If it wasn't love, it was something very like it.

'I…I don't want you to go,' she said in a tight

little voice. 'I would like to be friends…forget about the past.'

He shook his head. 'You've just told me the truth about how you felt when I ended our affair, Sally. I can't believe you can change your feelings for me so quickly.'

'But I know I can, Jack. I know the tragedy that lay behind what you did now.' She swallowed, and said almost in surprise, 'I don't dislike you, Jack. I know you're a good doctor and I…I like working with you.' Then she added softly, 'Please don't go…'

His eyes searched her face, held her steadfast gaze, then gradually his grave expression relaxed, making him look younger and more boyish. 'And I like working with you,' he murmured.

He nearly reached out to take her hand, but resisted the temptation. Any more physical contact with Sally and he would be lost. They couldn't begin a romance again, starting where they'd left off, could they? Things had changed. Now she knew he was the son of a murderer, would she really want to have an intimate relationship with him—and would it be fair to her? Of course it wouldn't. Romance was not on the cards, however much he yearned for her. Theirs would be a strictly professional relationship.

'Are you sure about this, Sally? You think we can get along OK until Jean comes back? In a purely working capacity, of course,' he added quickly.

'Yes…in a purely working capacity,' she murmured.

They looked at each other gravely in agreement then gradually their locked gazes intensified. Sally's mouth went dry and her heart began to beat an uncomfortable tattoo against her ribs. How could she ever have hated Jack? It was as if the unhappy years were melting away, and all the churning emotions she had felt over the past few weeks had crystallised into one overpowering thought—she wanted this man desperately, wanted to feel his arms around her again, his lips on hers once more.

Jack's eyes darkened, unable to hide the naked desire he felt for her, and he pushed his chair away, his voice husky, 'Why don't we have one last dance, then—just to celebrate our renewed friendship?'

'It's late…we'll miss the ferry.' Her mouth was dry. She wanted to dance with him like crazy but knew that if she did, any pretence of merely tolerating him would vanish.

'We've time,' Jack murmured confidently, pulling her against him once more.

He held her without speaking, and in the half-light of the room, amongst all the other couples, all Sally could see was the outline of that firm profile above her. His hard frame pressed urgently against her, hip to hip, and her body responded as if a switch had been thrown. She could feel how aroused he was…and she trembled because this time she knew that the shattering attraction she felt for him wasn't just one-sided.

He still wanted her as he had done all those years ago—and she wasn't surprised when he put his face down to hers and touched her lips with his, softly at first then more intrusively, teasing them apart, kissing the little hollow in her throat then tracing a path of fire down her neck… In the darkness his hand felt for the soft fullness of her breast, and a thousand butterflies seemed to flutter somewhere inside her. She wound her arms around his neck and allowed herself to relax against him. His hands held her head, pulling her face toward him, and his mouth claimed hers in a sweet, penetrating kiss that was stamped with sexual need and the clear message that he wanted more than this… much, much more. And she knew that without a doubt they'd both stepped over the line from formal colleagues to something much more intimate.

And all the way back on the ferry, as it chugged towards the flickering lights of Crannoch, he held her in his arms.

'Didn't you think La Famiglia was a great place?' demanded Sharon, tottering in with a pile of correspondence for Sally to look at. 'We had so much fun, but I'm so sorry that you and Jack had to wait for the later ferry—you must have felt very flat after we'd all left!'

'We managed to keep the conversation going,'

said Sally, trying to suppress a smile and re-
flecting that it had turned out to be a much
more interesting evening than she could have
envisaged!

'Well, you look much better for your night
out, I must say—really blooming,' observed
Sharon, looking at Sally critically and plonking
the letters on the desk. 'We've all thought you
looked so tired recently—probably pre-wedding
nerves, I suppose!'

'Er...probably,' murmured Sally, opening the
first letter in the pile Sharon had put down.

'It was such a shame your fiancé couldn't have
come with you,' Sharon prattled on, opening
and shutting a filing cabinet to put papers in.
'But the party was a good "last fling" before
your marriage, wasn't it? That's what puts me
off marriage—being joined hip to hip all the
time with the same man could be really boring!'

Sally sighed. She would have to tell everyone
soon that she and Tim weren't going to get married. At the moment the fact they thought she
was still engaged acted as a smokescreen for
her new relationship with Jack—but she wasn't

ready yet to announce that she and Jack were an item so soon after finishing with Tim. It was early days and there was still so much they had to talk about.

Last night had been like a new beginning, and it had happened so quickly. One minute she was telling Jack what a rat he'd been and how miserable he'd made her and then...then they'd almost fallen into each other's arms on the dance floor. After all the angst she'd been through, the feeling of rejection and the kaleidoscope of emotions from hatred to bewilderment that she'd felt, now there was an amazing relief that he finally trusted her enough to tell the truth. At last she knew why he'd had to get away, why he'd felt he couldn't bring all that baggage to their relationship.

God, she felt sorry for Jack—what he'd gone through. The disbelief there must have been, first, witnessing the terrible accident, and then watching his own father leave the scene whilst the girl lay dead in the road. Sally could imagine Jack's devastation, his total inability to reveal to her what had happened—how he would have done anything to keep her at a distance from the tragedy.

Even worse, in many ways, was his mother's rejection of him—blaming him for the fact his father was in jail. How could she cut him off, refuse to speak to him again? How bitter and sad Jack must feel about that.

But last night it had been as if they had been starting out all over again, with all the pulsating excitement of a first date. Jack had taken her back to the cottage and waited while she'd unlocked the door, then had put his arms on the newel post, imprisoning her between them. His kiss had been long and lingering, then he'd gently pulled aside the sleeves of her dress so that it had fallen from her shoulders and his mouth had moved down her neck and to her breasts with light butterfly kisses—just as he'd done years ago, and just as she had once done she had responded passionately, as if making up for the years they'd been apart.

'God, Sally, how beautiful you are, and how I've longed to do this, ' he'd said huskily, burying his face in her sweet-smelling hair, his mouth becoming more and demanding on hers. Then he'd pulled back for a second, the old cheeky persuasiveness twinkling in his eyes. 'You know what? It would be easier to see you properly inside the cottage…and a bit more comfortable!'

How simple it would have been to easy to fall into bed with him—to finish this amazing evening in the most romantic way possible—but for some reason a little shred of prudence held her back.

'Hey there,' she'd said, smiling. 'One step at a time. I've waited quite a few years for this moment so I can wait a little while longer.'

He'd pulled back, trailed a finger down her jaw and stroked her thick, soft hair. 'I can't believe I'm saying this, but perhaps you're right—let's take all the time we can.'

Then he'd kissed her lips softly again and made his way back to the car.

Sally sat at her desk, oblivious to Sharon's noisy opening and shutting of filing cabinets, in a happy world of her own, reliving last night like the rewinding of a wonderfully romantic

film. She would see Jack after work tonight—
she'd ask him at lunchtime if he wanted to go
for a walk and have a meal with her later—get
to know each other all over again. Suddenly life
was exciting and full of possibilities. She felt
so happy and alive, but nervous too. She and
Jack had a second chance and she didn't want
anything to spoil it.

'Full surgery this morning,' remarked Sharon
with a final bang of several drawers.

Sally came to with a start. She was acting
like a star-struck teenager, in love for the very
first time, she thought guiltily. She had to pull
herself together and concentrate on her patients
and not fall into a happy daze every time she
thought of Jack! She brought up the list of that
morning's patients and saw with pleasure that
the first on the list was Ian Kershaw. He was
an outward bound instructor who ran a school
for children with special needs up the coast,
and had booked to have a large mole removed
from his arm if Sally thought it was necessary.
He was a good friend of hers and she was the

appointed doctor for the school—she really wanted Jack to meet him.

'Normally I wouldn't have bothered you, Sally,' said Ian, 'but I read an article about skin cancer and thought I'd better have you look at this mole.'

'Quite right,' agreed Sally, as she swabbed Ian's arm and anaesthetised the skin with a local injection. 'Nowadays we should be much more aware of the damage sun can do—especially someone like you with very fair, freckly skin, which is more sensitive to sun damage.'

'Do you think it's cancerous?' asked Ian.

'It looks harmless, but I'm sending it for a biopsy just to make sure…'

Carefully she cut along the natural folds of the skin to produce a good cosmetic result, and with a pair of small tweezers put the removed mole into a sterile container.

'Now I'll just put in a few stitches. I shan't use dissolving ones because on the surface they can cause lumpy scars… There! You're blemish-free now! Come back in four days to have those stitches out, and you'll be perfect!'

'Thanks, Sally.' He put on his shirt and jacket again. 'You are coming to the fun fair day we're having at the school next week, aren't you? It's to raise money for the special needs playground we're trying to get started. I've got some leaflets here.'

'Of course. Tell Jean and she'll put them on the tables in the waiting room and we'll put one up on the notice-board.'

'That would be great. Tell all your friends to come as well. We've got that film star Careena Fox to come and open the fair—not often there are any celebrities in this area, but apparently the place is full of them at the moment!'

'I'll be there!' Sally smiled, thinking that she would get Jack to go with her. He would be interested to see the school and the marvellous work they did with the children, and even more interested to see how their patient had improved since her brush with the dreaded giant hog-weed! She threw the needle and tiny scalpel she'd been using into the sharps bin and flicked a look at the list of morning patients. Still a long way to go before a coffee break and the chance to see Jack again. After a typical morning of sore throats, bad backs and children with hacking coughs she went down the corridor to Jack's room and knocked on his door.

Jack looked up and grinned, his eyes dancing mischievously at her. 'Now the morning's certainly improved. I presume you want a consultation? I'll be very happy to examine you…'

He rose from his seat and strode across to her, putting his hands on her shoulders and pulling her towards him. 'Let me see,' he murmured, looking down at her face, laughter in the depths of his blue eyes. 'First of all, a lip examination…'

He bent his head to hers and kissed her gently but firmly on her parted lips. She tried to resist for a second or two, but she couldn't help responding, melting into him, revelling in the salty taste of his lips and the feel of his muscular body against hers. Then, as if realising where they were, she pulled back with a guilty little giggle.

'Hey, we're at work, you know!'

'Nonsense! It's just what the doctor ordered.

You know what they say…all work and no play, etcetera. You don't want me to be a dull man, do you? And by the way, your lips are one hundred per cent perfect!' His expression changed slightly, his open, strong face gravely tender as he brushed away a lock of hair over her forehead. 'Was that a wonderful night last night or what?' he murmured. 'I haven't felt so happy for a long time. To know that you don't hate me so much after all…'

'I suppose I quite like you really,' she teased, pulling away from him, sitting on the side of the desk and swinging her legs. 'How about going on a nice walk and then me making you a meal afterwards tonight?' she asked him.

'I like the sound of that…especially the "afterwards" bit…'

'And there's something else—will you come with me at the weekend to the special needs school near here? They're having a fun day to raise money and a friend of mine works there who I'd like you to meet.'

'Sure.'

The phone rang just then and he picked up

the receiver. Sally watched Jack's face change as he listened to the caller. After a short conversation he put the phone down. 'You'll never guess who that was—it was that lovely old lady, Hilda Brown, the one who lives up at the house on the hill.'

'Is she all right?'

'She's got her solicitor and an estate agent with her, and wants us to sign some papers—it sounds as if it could be something to do with her daughter.' He looked enquiringly at Sally. 'Perhaps now would be a good time? We've got some space before afternoon clinics so we'll have a bite of lunch as well.'

'A good idea. I wonder what's been going on between Hilda and her daughter?'

A few minutes later they were once more on the road to The Chase, Mrs Brown's house up in the hills. He stopped outside a little corner store at the edge of the village.

'Won't be a second—just need to buy a few things,' he said, dashing into the shop.

He came out with a bulging plastic bag, which he put into the boot before driving on.

'It doesn't seem six weeks ago that we were going to see this lady,' he murmured. He flicked a mischievous glance at Sally. 'I remember smelling the perfume you use and it bringing back memories of when we used to be together—of how six years ago we'd end up making love after a hard day's work. I never thought it might happen again…' Their eyes met briefly and there was mutual passion and desire in that swift glance.

'Jack McLennan, keep your thoughts on your work,' said Sally primly, but inside her heart was galloping with the excitement of knowing that sooner or later they would make love, and it would be as if they had never parted at all.

There were two cars already parked in front of the house, and when they went to the door it was opened by a woman with a crutch in one hand and a leg encased in a cast. Her face seemed slightly familiar. She smiled up at the two doctors.

'Don't you remember me?' she asked. 'I'm Geraldine Foster—I was involved in that traffic accident a few weeks ago and you were the doctors looking after me. You were ever so kind!'

'Of course!' cried Sally. 'We were called in to help at the hospital that day. I remember you were going to start a new job here that day. You're actually working here now?'

'Only very light duties at the moment,' explained Geraldine. 'But Mrs Brown and I get on like a house on fire. I love helping her, she's such a wonderful lady. Will you come through to the drawing room?'

She led the way to the beautiful room with its marvellous view over the sea to the island. The room looked rather different: there was no clutter over the floor; the papers had been tidied away; and there was no sign of dirty crockery. A huge bowl of sweet peas had been placed on a pretty little oak table and their delicate fragrance filled the room. The wooden corner cupboards had been polished until their surfaces gleamed.

'I can see you've made a difference to the place already, Geraldine,' murmured Jack appreciatively.

Mrs Brown, however, looked much the same if a little frailer—a small figure in a wing chair with a jumble of clothes on, a brilliant red wrap over a long blue skirt, and again a hat at a jaunty angle on her head. By her side stood two men drinking coffee, one of whom Jack recognised as the first patient he'd seen when he'd joined the practice.

'Ah, the doctors. Thank you so much for coming over,' she called out when she saw Jack and Sally. 'Sit down, my dears. I have much that I want to talk to you about.' She introduced the two men. 'This is my solicitor, Edwin Brotherton, and this is Angus Knightley, our local estate agent…'

'Aye, I know Dr McLennan,' said Angus with a broad smile. 'He did wonders for me—I feel better than I have done for years! Thank you, Doctor!'

Jack smiled. 'I'm glad to say you look a new man, Mr Knightley.'

Hilda tapped on a little table. 'Now, let's get down to business. Basically I want you doctors to confirm that I am not mad, bad or stupid

because I want to put the house on the market—
and I don't want my daughter saying I'm not in
my right mind to do so!'

Sally looked in surprise at the old lady. 'But
you love living here, don't you? And now you've
got help, surely it's easier for you?'

Hilda nodded, and said briskly, 'Yes, I adore
The Chase—my husband and I were blissfully
happy here for many, many years. But I've got
to be sensible. The place is vast for one person.
There are rooms here I haven't seen for years,
and in the last few weeks I've realised I'm getting weaker. I want to move before it's too much
for me. I don't want the place to deteriorate. It's
a house for a family. It should be ringing with
children's laughter, not mouldering away with
the dust of old age and neglect.'

'Mrs Brown wants to sell the house and move
to a cottage Mr Knightley has found for her in
the village, looking over the sound,' explained
Edwin Brotherton.

'I see…I thought…I thought…' Sally faltered,
slightly embarrassed to put her thoughts into
words.

'You thought my daughter wanted the house?'

guessed Hilda shrewdly. 'As I think I told you before, I have given Mary a large amount of money in my time—and her father left her well provided for. Together she and her husband have frittered it away on a variety of projects. I don't believe they would look after the house properly—they have a habit of letting things go. When I die she'll come into even more money, but I want to see this dear old place go to a responsible owner—someone who will grow to love it as I do.'

'Have you told your daughter this?' asked Jack.

'Mary and I have had a falling out over it. She thinks I'm out of my mind.' Hilda looked sharply at Sally and Jack. 'I wouldn't put it past Mary to mention it to you—and that's why I want you to certify in the presence of my solicitor that I'm not daft in the head!'

'So when would you move? It could take some time to sell the house,' remarked Sally.

'Mrs Brown has already bought the cottage so could move any time, and I know that although this house needs some attention, it is unique and will attract many prospective buyers,' said Mr Knightley.

'I know it will,' murmured Jack. 'It must be in one of the finest positions in the country.' He smiled at Hilda. 'It's going to be a wrench, but I'm sure you'll love living in the village—you know so many people there.'

"Right!' declared the old lady. 'Now, let's ask Geraldine to get us all some fresh coffee and some of her delicious scones while we get down to business!'

'I can't believe that Hilda wants to give up her beautiful home,' said Sally as they drove back down the winding road. 'You'd have thought she would have wanted to end her days there.'

'I think she wanted to keep control of the place—decide who she wanted to sell it to before she died, and not leave it to the tender mercies of Mary Olsen and her husband,' Jack remarked. 'It's sad that mother and daughter don't get on but I really don't feel sorry for Mary Olsen—she won't be left destitute.' He flicked a look at Sally and grinned. 'Anyway, it's too nice a day to worry about the Olsens or anything else to do with medicine—let's go and have some lunch where I can talk to you and look at you. We've got an hour before we go back.'

Sally hugged her arms to herself, trying to contain the shivering little darts of excitement that were happening when she was with Jack. An hour to themselves, thinking of nothing but each other…

He swung off the road and down a small farm track with wide fields on either side. 'This is a little place I found when I took a wrong turn to see a patient about ten days ago,' he remarked. 'I hope you like it.'

Sally was expecting to see a little out-of-the-way pub as they bumped their way down the steep track, but when they got to the bottom they had reached a small sandy cove, completely sheltered by cliffs.

'Oh, Jack—this is lovely!' breathed Sally, getting out of the car and taking in a deep breath of the tangy scent of the sea as she looked around. 'I never knew it existed!'

The sun was out and the air was warm and fresh on her face and there was the mingled smell of wild thyme and rosemary carried on the warm breeze that whispered over the cliff tops. She looked around with delight. The craggy cliff was scattered with flashes of blue where cornflowers had flowered and small sea pinks made a cushion over the more rocky places.

'Jack, this is magic...'

'I know!' he said modestly. 'But I'm even cleverer than you thought—if you sit down here, madam, on this rug, I will now provide a mouth-watering repast especially for you!'

He laid down a rug on the soft sand of the little beach and Sally sat on it, looking at the sea glinting and sparkling in the sun. It was like a dream—a beautiful setting on a summer's day with the man she had fallen in love with all over again.

She looked across at him walking towards her, tall, rangy and drop-dead handsome, his hair blowing in the slight breeze, a carefree grin on his face, and her heart bounded with happiness—she could hardly believe that a few days ago she'd been so miserable and confused. And all it had taken had been for Jack to tell her the truth—terrible though it was—for her to understand how torn he must have been. She felt a sudden constriction in her throat as she thought of the young man driven out of the family by his own mother, never to speak to her again or to be shown any forgiveness for handing his father over to the police. What a hard road he'd had to walk, keeping his sadness to himself. In many ways it had been a brave decision to leave for Australia, cutting himself off from family and friends—but it had kept them apart for six years.

Jack dumped the plastic bag on the ground and sat by her side.

'And now for the first of the Crannoch stores delights—this is Chateau Crannoch,' he said, pulling out two plastic beakers and a bottle of white wine. 'I'm not too sure of the vintage, but let's give it a go…' He poured them each a drink and smiled at her. 'To us both, my love,' he murmured.

They both took a sip and then simultaneously

grimaced. 'What's it made of?' spluttered Sally. 'It's like vinegar!'

'Probably is.' Jack smiled. 'Ah, well…let's try the next sumptuous offering…' He pulled out of the bag a plastic-encased sandwich. 'Corned beef and lettuce cordon bleu,' he pronounced. 'The best that the local shop has to offer.'

He gave Sally a half and he took the other half. Sally looked down at hers. It didn't look very appetising—the bread was white and soggy and the lettuce wilting.

Jack laughed and stuffed his food back in the bag. 'I think you'd have to be very hungry to want to eat this! What shall we do?'

He put his hand under her chin and turned her face towards him, his twinkling blue eyes looking into hers. Then slowly his expression changed to a burning look of desire and he pulled her down on the rug so that she was lying beside him. Sally's heart began to thump against her ribs—she knew what was going to happen and she wasn't going to do a thing to stop it… Jack had once caused her so much unhappiness, but he'd finished with her because of the terrible thing that had happened to his family. She understood that. Now they could put the past behind them and suddenly there seemed to be a wonderful future in front of her with someone who loved her. What a pale imitation of love she and Tim had had in comparison with what she felt for Jack now.

She put her arms round his neck and pulled him close to her. 'I know what we can do,' she whispered.

He stroked her silky hair back from her forehead, looking down at the sweep of her eyelashes against the peachy skin, her full soft mouth and high cheek bones, and he smiled mischievously. 'I wonder if it's what I want to do too?' he murmured. 'The thing is that suddenly I have got an appetite, Sally, darling, but not for food...'

Then his mouth covered hers with a long passionate kiss, and he lay over her, his hard muscular frame against her soft curves, and he murmured huskily, 'God, how long have I dreamt of doing this with you again...' He laughed. 'Do you think we can remember how to do it, sweetheart?'

Sally giggled. 'If I remember, we normally took our clothes off before we...'

'Glad you reminded me.' Then he bent his head down, and his mouth was on hers, setting her lips on fire, melting them in a long passionate kiss. 'Sally, you're so beautiful,' he murmured. 'Every little bit of you...'

And then under the warm summer sun he made love to her on the soft beach, their bodies melded together, limbs entwined, his body hard and demanding, hers soft and yielding, revelling in the waves of sweetness that swept through them. And it was just as wild and wonderful as it had been six years before. The memories of how he'd made love to her came flooding back—his special gentleness, the way he led her to unimagined heights of passion when every erogenous zone in her body responded to his skilful touch...his tender murmurings...

'This was how it used to be between us,' he whispered. 'This and this and this...'

And afterwards, as they lay curled round each

other with the waves lapping on the shore beside them, he told her how he'd longed for her all the time he'd been in Australia, but had never been able to bear to make contact with her because of his shame at what had happened in his family.

'There was no point in writing to you—I thought I could never come home. My mother disowned me. I'd broken the trust of the family.'

Sally stroked Jack's springy hair back from his forehead. 'How could she do that to you? Did she never make contact?'

He laughed bitterly. 'I did get two letters—I never opened them. I couldn't bear her accusations of betrayal…and perhaps, looking at it from her point of view, I had broken up the family.' Then he sat up and looked down at her. 'But we're not going to talk about it anymore, sweetheart…we're going to look forward.'

'It's a fresh start, isn't it?' Sally murmured, her clear grey eyes smiling dreamily at him. 'We've got years and years ahead of us, haven't we?'

Funny how mobile phones seemed programmed to ring at the most inappropriate moments, thought Sally as its familiar tone rang loudly inside her bag. She made a face at Jack. 'Sorry,' she said, 'I'd better get it—it could be the surgery.' She winked at him and then said vivaciously into the phone, 'Hi, Mum! No, of course it's not inconvenient! I was just…er… enjoying myself with a friend. Yes, that would be great—I'd love to see you on Sunday. OK. Love you both!'

Jack looked at her heart-shaped face and wide grey eyes as she listened to her mother. Sally had a kind of radiance about her and a warm beauty she was quite unconscious of… no wonder her parents adored her. It must be wonderful to have a loving relationship like that with your mother, he thought wistfully. How different Sally's and his experiences of childhood had been. She had been a cherished child in a stable home—he had been an unhappy boy growing up in an atmosphere of violence and distrust.

A tiny seed of doubt began to form in his mind. Had he been totally selfish, making love to Sally—a vulnerable woman who'd so recently just broken off her engagement? In the cold light of day how would she feel about being with the son of a murderer and all the background baggage he brought with him? Sally was so trusting of him, and now they'd crossed some kind of Rubicon. They were finally lovers again, and it had been wonderful, unbelievable. But it had all happened so quickly. Twenty-four hours ago Sally had hated him, and now they were together, locked in each other's arms. No time to draw breath, no time to discuss what their future might be.

Jack rolled on his back and stared up at the blue sky. Circumstances had made him cynical and after six years they were two very different people. What Sally hoped for, expected, might be very different to his ideas, because, if he was honest, he was wary of marriage—in his experience of two warring parents, it didn't lead to happiness. Indeed, marriage to him meant two people being locked together in a prison of unhappiness. He knew he loved Sally, but he was very unsure whether he wanted to get married—and was that being fair to her?

He couldn't let her down again, lead her on with expectations of happy-ever-after that he might never be able to fulfil.

CHAPTER NINE

IT WAS time to tell everyone at work that she was not engaged anymore to Tim, Sally decided as she parked her car the next day, although she rather dreaded the furore of comment and discussion that would probably happen. She was certainly not going to announce to the world yet that she and Jack were now an item, their rediscovered romance was still too new, but every now and then a little thrill of happiness rippled through her as she thought back to making love with Jack by the sea on a warm afternoon… something she'd thought would never happen again.

Sally wanted to hug this wonderful secret to herself for a while, not be under the spotlight of curious staff or patients. It was one thing to break off an engagement—it was another to announce that she was now in a relationship

with someone else. It was slightly embarrassing that she seemed to leap from man to man
rather quickly! And, of course, she thought
wryly, there were her parents to consider. How
would they take the information that she was
going out again with the man they thought had
destroyed her life at one time? That was going
to need careful handling…

She went into the office where Sharon and
Joyce were sitting drinking cups of coffee and
poring over a travel brochure.

'Hi, everyone,' she sang out. 'I think I'll have
a strong cup of that…'

Joyce handed her a cup and said gloom-
ily, 'You're going to be busy today—there's a
crowded vaccination clinic and then you've both
got the primary care trust meeting this afternoon.'

As Sally had predicted, several cases of measles had been confirmed amongst the children
at the nursery school that Charlie Fleming at-
tended and now parents were clamouring to
have their children vaccinated.

'Ah, well, perhaps Jack can give me an hour if

Sula can't help. We'll get through it somehow, and the meeting isn't until later.' In her present happy mood Sally felt she could cope with anything. 'Are you planning some holidays?' she enquired, glancing at the brochure they were looking at.

'I want to go somewhere really lively,' announced Sharon. 'And I'm trying to persuade Joyce to do more than go to her cousin's in Paisley.' She looked enviously at Sally. 'Lucky you, going on honeymoon soon. Do you know where you're going?'

Sally took a deep breath. Sharon had given her a good opening to reveal what had happened between her and Tim. 'Actually, girls,' she said rather haltingly, 'I've something to tell you. Perhaps I should have told you this a while ago. The thing is, Tim and I have been thinking things over and we've decided that perhaps we shouldn't get married after all. We've broken off our engagement.'

Both women looked at her in astonishment, then Sharon said in a small voice, 'D'you mean there won't be a wedding? We won't get to wear our outfits?'

'For goodness' sake, girl,' snapped Joyce. 'Is that all you can think of?' She went over to Sally and put her hand on her arm, looking at her shrewdly. 'I'm sorry, lass, you must have been through a lot of sadness. I've been thinking lately you've not been your usual happy self, although you certainly look brighter today. But if Tim's not the right man then it's for the best, isn't it?'

Sally smiled gratefully—Joyce was a plain-speaking woman but had a heart of gold. 'To tell you the truth, it's a relief. Tim's going to get married to his secretary and I'm not heartbroken at all. It just came to a mutual end, that's all.'

'Well, I'm not giving up hope of still wearing that outfit,' said Sharon stoutly. 'You'll meet someone again very soon, I'm sure of it.'

Sally examined the cover of a medical magazine on the desk very closely to hide the slight blush on her face.

'I don't think I'll plunge into another engage-ment just yet,' she said lightly.

She went into her room with her coffee to start going through some of her e-mails. She draped her jacket over her chair and turned on her computer, humming happily to herself as she waited for it to boot up. She couldn't wait to see Jack again to talk about some of the lovely things they might do together.

It was near lunchtime and the morning surgery had finished. Jack put two aspirins in his mouth and swallowed them down with a glass of water. He had a thumping headache, brought on he knew by his underlying worries about his rela-tionship with Sally and if she'd really thought through being in a relationship with him now she knew about his history. By a terrible irony his last patient that morning had helped to bring these worries to the surface. Little did Nesta Grahame realise that her story had triggered terrible memories of Jack's life when he'd been young.

The young woman was thin, pale and poorly

dressed with unkempt hair—and very heavily pregnant. Sharon had brought her in and helped her to sit down on the chair in front of Jack's desk.

'This is Nesta Grahame,' Sharon had announced. 'She was found outside the surgery on the pavement feeling unwell. She says she's OK. But Joyce said she ought to be looked at.'

Jack had run a quick visual check on Nesta, experience telling him that her dry hair, redness round the eyes and the cracked, spoon-shaped nails on the hand she placed on the desk could be caused by iron-deficiency anaemia. He would have bet on it that she'd never been for any antenatal check-ups—she'd had the neglected air of someone who didn't look after herself.

'I was just a bit faint—that's all,' the young woman had muttered rather defensively. 'I was trying to get my breath. I'll be all right. I'm pregnant, see?'

Jack had smiled at her. 'I certainly do see. Will you let me examine you just to check that things are OK, like blood pressure, urine, and to see if the baby's in a good position?'

'No!' she'd said sharply. 'I don't want that… just give me a tonic or something that'll stop this dizzy feeling.'

'I think you're probably anaemic. I can give you some iron tablets but I would like to do a blood test to make sure. A few drops of blood from your arm…'

Nesta got up quickly from the chair and glared at Jack. 'No, I'm OK. Just give me the tablets…'

She swayed for a moment, then put her hand to her head and crumpled slowly to the floor. Jack sprinted round the desk and managed to haul her into a sitting position with her head bent over her knees, and in doing so he pulled up her sleeves from her wrists.

'Oh, hell,' he whispered, staring at her thin, bare arms in horror. They were covered with bruises, some old and yellow, some dark and recent. Like a rerun of a film, it brought back a vivid picture of many years ago when he'd been a little boy and had gone to hug his mother. He remembered how she'd winced as he'd clutched her arms—just like Nesta's, they'd been covered in bruises. Nesta didn't want to be examined, he thought grimly, because she was trying to conceal her injuries.

A hot cup of tea laced with sugar seemed to restore Nesta's spirits somewhat and she seemed more willing to talk as the sweet liquid gave her an energy boost.

'I'd like you to go for a check-up at the gynae clinic at the hospital,' Jack said, scribbling a note on a pad. 'Your baby's fine, I'm sure, but I'm suggesting a day or two's stay while they run tests on you, build you up a bit. A little tender loving care won't do you any harm.' He paused for a moment and said gently, 'You've got a lot of bruises and cuts—how did you get those?'

He looked at Nesta very kindly and the automatic denial she was about to give petered out in the face of his gentleness. Jack guessed Nesta didn't receive much kindness in her life. She bit her lip and looked down at her lap.

'Kirk didn't mean no harm,' she said defiantly. 'He's lost his job, see—and so he had too many drinks. That's what does it—the drink. It makes him get angry... He can't help it, says I wind him up.'

Jack nodded calmly, not wanting her to think he was moralising, but he'd guessed as much. 'Is Kirk your partner, then?'

'He's my husband,' Nesta said with a certain amount of misplaced pride. 'But I'm not leaving him—and I'm not reporting him,' she added quickly. 'He's OK without the booze.' She looked mutinously at Jack. 'But you wouldn't understand. It's not his fault...'

Oh, but I would understand, thought Jack savagely. He remembered his mother's mantra, that it was never his father's fault that he abused her, bullied the children and generally ruined their family life. Nesta was a young version of his mother—another life that would be ruined because somehow he knew that Nesta wouldn't leave this man or ever press charges.

After she'd gone, clutching the note he'd given her for the hospital, Jack walked over to the window and watched her pathetic little figure waddle slowly over to the bus stop. Poor woman.

She was in for a lifetime of unhappiness, and he had no doubt that the child she had would be abused just like he had been.

He turned with an impatient gesture and sat down at the desk. It wasn't a new scenario. There were plenty of Nestas out there, and he empathised with them. But today…today was different because Nesta's plight had a bearing on his life now. In the cold light of day, after they'd made love, perhaps Sally would think she didn't want to be with the son of a drunkard, a murderer. And every time they had a disagreement, would she wonder if he was taking after his father?

He stared bleakly ahead of him. Perhaps he'd spoken the truth when he'd declared to her that he wasn't marriage material. He and Sally had leapt over the boundary of colleagues to lovers so quickly, and he'd been like an express train running out of control, unable to resist the crackling attraction between them after the years of loneliness and longing to be with her. It had happened so suddenly, so overwhelmingly that reason and sense had flown out of the window.

His mother had told Jack that he'd betrayed his family, that he was a traitor. Reason told him that he'd done the right thing, but love for his mother made him feel that he was in large part responsible for the family break-up. That was what being brought up in a drunkard's family did to you. It twisted your logic, made you feel guilty although it wasn't your fault. He shook his head bitterly. How could he think that he and Sally could start up their relationship again with no thought of the problems he bought with him? It was hard to believe in an institution that had only brought him and his brother misery.

The meeting was long and tedious that afternoon, with representatives of all the primary trust general practitioners gathered to discuss networking the computer system so that they could communicate effectively with each other and the hospitals in the area. Sally did her best to concentrate, but her mind was definitely not focussed on computer systems that afternoon.

Her thoughts kept sliding back to the marvellous afternoon the day before, rerunning the sweetness of making love with Jack, hardly able to believe all that had happened within twenty-four hours.

There was just the faintest dark cloud on her horizon. She had assumed that Jack and she would drive to the meeting together—it was about half an hour away from Crannoch—but after the clinic, where they'd been far too busy to talk to each other, he'd e-mailed her to say that he would go under his own steam after all. He'd mentioned rather vaguely that he had to get away after the meeting to see his brother so he needed his own car. Sally couldn't help feeling slightly put out that he hadn't asked her to go along with him—she'd like to have met his brother.

There was a short question-and-answer session at the end of the meeting and Sally looked across the room. She'd kept a chair beside her for Jack, but he obviously hadn't noticed it and was sitting at the other side of the room from her. Poor darling, she thought fondly, he looked really tired. Perhaps yesterday afternoon had exhausted him, she thought with a little inward giggle. She watched him, ready to smile and wave, but he didn't look up, and the meeting drew to a close.

Sally got up, clutching a sheaf of notes in her hand, and made her way over to him, determined to make him have a cup of tea with her before he left to see his brother. There was a tap on her shoulder as she pushed through the crowd of people and a jolly voice said, 'It's Sally Lawson, isn't it? Hi, Sally, haven't seen you in an age. How are things?'

Sally whipped round to see a short, fair woman standing next to her and after a second's look she gave an astonished whoop of surprise. 'Oh, my God! Lorna Sanders! How marvellous to see you! I can't believe it! It must be six years since we worked together…St Mary's A and E?'

'Those were the days, eh?' Lorna grinned. They hugged each other and Lorna put her hands on Sally's shoulders and looked at her appraisingly. 'Still as gorgeous as ever, I see. How dare you still look so young? Not a wrinkle in sight! Now, I don't care what you say—you and I are having a cup of tea right now and catching up with each other.' She put a hand up to prevent any objection from Sally. 'Don't say you can't. Everyone's got to eat. You can get back to work later!'

'Well…I'm actually trying to get hold of…' Sally looked across the room towards Jack, but rather to her disappointment he'd disappeared. She was a little surprised that he'd not come over to say goodbye—he must have been in a great hurry to see his brother.

She turned back to Lorna with a smile. They'd got on very well in A and E. However stressful it had been, you could rely on Lorna to be cheerful and fun—and full of gossip. For a year or two they'd sent Christmas cards with scrappy bits of news in them, but life had been busy and Lorna had worked in London and they'd somehow drifted apart.

Lorna pulled her into a little café and they sat down near the window. 'Isn't this wonderful?' She beamed at Sally. 'I never dreamed I'd see you here. We'll have a discreet glass of wine each to toast our meeting!'

'And you must be working in this area now? I thought you'd never leave London,' remarked Sally.

'When I got married, my husband Ron, who comes from around here, joined a practice about ten miles away, and I'm working with him now. I really love it here—and now I know you're in the area it'll be the icing on the cake.' Lorna leaned forward and fixed Sally with a beady eye. 'Now...' she grinned '...tell me all. What happened to you after that twerp Jack McLennan went off Down Under? I could never believe what he did to you!'

Lorna always was direct, thought Sally wryly. 'I got a job here as a GP,' she said. 'It took me some time to get over it—but I survived.'

'I knew you would...you're one sparky girl. You're better off without him anyway!' Lorna paused and shook her head sadly, 'I have to say, though, Jack really fooled me. I thought he was a fabulous man and that you made a great couple.'

'Perhaps he wasn't so bad,' hedged Sally. 'Actually,' she began cautiously, unwilling to divulge just yet the precise relationship between her and Jack—she could hardly believe it herself! 'By a curious coincidence he's back here and working in my practice!'

'Is he indeed?' Lorna looked at her in surprise. 'So he turned up again like a bad penny. I hope you'll be careful this time not to get involved—once bitten, twice shy, eh? He's just the sort of drop-dead-gorgeous guy who leaves a trail of broken-hearted women behind him.'

'Jack had very good reasons for leaving me,' said Sally stoutly.

'Well, you once told me it was because he wanted to further his career—but I don't believe that. It just doesn't ring true to me. If you ask me, that was just an excuse, going all the way to Australia. I guess he was just terrified of commitment, like a lot of men, and, charming or not, too cowardly to make the leap!'

Sally opened her mouth to protest that she knew what had really happened, then thought better of it. Lorna would believe what she wanted to, whatever Sally's explanation.

Lorna shook her finger at Sally. 'Believe me, a leopard never changes his spots, honey. He's the sort that will always run away from commitment.' Then she grinned and raised her glass. 'Anyway, let's not talk about Jack. Here's to the two of us. Have you heard from any of the others we used to work with?'

And then they were on to safer ground as they talked about old colleagues. But as she drove home, Lorna's words seemed to echo in Sally's mind and she felt a certain irritation with her old friend. She knew the truth about Jack now and the terrible thing that had caused him to go to Australia, and she was utterly sure that now they'd got together again they'd be together for good—of course they would.

As she drove into the surgery car park Sally saw Jack's car parked at the end of the row and Jack was just getting out of the car. Like a reflex action, she felt her pulse quicken when she saw him, a ripple of excitement flickering through her body. She still could hardly believe that after all this time their romance had kick-started again. His thick hair was rumpled and from the back his shoulders drooped wearily, but he was one fabulous guy. She closed her eyes for a second, savouring the wonderful memory of their love-making on the beach in the little cove that magical afternoon, his soft voice whispering how much he loved her, wanted her… She slammed the car door and ran up to him.

'Jack! I'm so glad to see you! I tried to find you after the meeting but you'd disappeared. Did you meet your brother?'

He turned round and with a slight shock she saw how grey his face looked, little lines of tiredness around his eyes.

'Are you OK? You look exhausted…'

Clear blue eyes stared at her for a moment and briefly she saw a kind of yearning in their depths, then suddenly it was as if a shutter had come down and all emotion was wiped from his face.

'Ah…Sally. I'm sorry I didn't let you know, but Liam was in Glasgow and I wanted to take the chance to see him.'

'Of course—but you look absolutely shattered. Why don't I make you a meal tonight?'

He hesitated a moment, then shook his head. 'Perhaps not tonight, Sally. I've got some sorting out to do, a few calls to make.'

Sally smiled at him. 'And that's going to take all evening? You still need to eat, don't you?'

By this time they were inside the practice and Jack stood at his doorway, looking down at her with an unreadable expression, then he sighed. 'Come into my room for a minute,' he said. 'I need a word with you.'

'Sounds rather serious,' joked Sally. 'Have I done something wrong?'

His voice was tight, controlled. 'Of course you haven't,' he said abruptly. He pushed a chair forward. 'Sit down.'

He paced up and down for a minute while Sally stared at him in bewilderment. Then he wheeled round and faced her. 'The truth is, Sally, I've been thinking about us…'

Sally dimpled at him. 'So have I.'

He put up his hand. 'Let me speak, sweetheart. God, this is difficult to say—you'll think

I'm doing a re-run of what happened before. But the fact is the past twenty-four hours have been like a dream—'

'There's a "but" here somewhere,' interjected Sally lightly.

'I'm just saying everything happened so quickly. Maybe we should take our time to consider the future more…'

Sally grew very still and began to feel cold. 'What the hell are you saying, Jack?' she whispered slowly. 'Come on, spit it out! If something's worrying you, you'd better tell me.'

Jack pulled up another chair, sat down on it and took her hands in his. 'Sally, darling, it's hard to say this, just when we'd got together again, but I don't think you've taken in the full implications: I'm the son of a drunk who killed someone—and I betrayed my own father. I cannot expect you to push that to the back of our relationship.'

'I don't care about that, Jack.'

'You say that now, but the past could come back to haunt me. Even now, after all these years, it still occupies my mind.' He looked at her grimly. 'I should never have come to work with you when we met a few weeks ago. I knew the pitfalls. I knew how attracted I still was to you…even after six years. In the cold light of day I think I have too much baggage to lumber you with. You need to get married to some-one who's got a clean slate, no complications in his past. Someone whose family comes from a similar stable background to yours.'

Sally pulled her hands away from his, sprang up from the chair and looked at him scornfully. 'The truth is you just don't want to commit to any woman, do you? When the going gets hot, you get cold feet. The plain fact is that you just don't want a steady partner or children—any-thing that means you might have to open up and confront your past, rather than keep running.'

'That's ridiculous,' he protested. 'Of course I want a family, but there are things about me, my background, that make me—'

'Afraid? Or is it just an excuse to be a phi-landerer?' Suddenly Lorna's words echoed in Sally's mind clearly. 'You've had your little fling with me again but as soon as any emotional commitment is required it's on to new pastures! Isn't that the truth of it?' A little break in her voice betrayed her shock and despair.

'No, that's not true at all. I've told you—the reality is that I'm damaged goods when it comes to happy-ever-after. Whatever my father did, my mother was right. I broke up our family and she couldn't forgive me for that. I won't be responsible for breaking up another family. Our family.'

His voice was flat but his expression was anguished as he forced the words out. He lifted her chin and gazed at her heart-shaped face, the wide grey eyes and their frames of long, dark lashes. 'Sally, sweetheart, in a few days you'll think about things and realise that a future with me would be a rocky thing. I betrayed my family…my mother, my father…and I still live with that guilt.'

Sally twisted her hands together. She didn't care what his family background was, she could only sympathise with him—but how could she convince him of that?

'So that's it, is it?' she whispered. 'You want to call it a day—again?'

'I need to allow you the freedom to live without me,' he said quietly. 'I think I was right before when I said I must leave the practice—I can't work beside you and not love you. When you've found a replacement for me, I'll get out of your life.'

The room seemed to rock. Sally rose from the chair, her face flushed, eyes bright with unshed tears, and stood in front of him, her hands making tight fists by her sides. She took a deep breath and said slowly and deliberately, 'Jack McLennan, you've done this once before to me and it broke my heart, but if you feel you can't commit to me then I'm not going to force you.' She was silent for a moment and then said sadly, 'I thought we loved each other and I thought you finally trusted me, that we could overcome the past together.'

She went out of the door and shut it quietly behind her. Jack sat down at the desk and put his head in his hands. What had he done? What the hell had he done? He loved Sally—had never stopped loving her—but with the mess that was his family background, and the terrible fear that always shadowed his life that he might have inherited his father's legacy, how could he ask her to take that on?

He couldn't bear the thought that two people who were once in love might end up hating each other, like his parents had.

CHAPTER TEN

THIS couldn't be happening—not again. Sally gazed at the shadows dancing on the ceiling above her, unable to get to sleep. Every night it had been the same—tossing and turning, trying to reconcile the fact that for a second time the man she loved had left her. For a horrible week they had been working in the same building, passing in the corridor, meeting in the office, but only communicating with a kind of stiff courtesy. And all the time she longed to feel his arms about her, longed to go up to him and hold her to him—but she wasn't going to plead. What was the point of yearning after someone who didn't want to commit himself to you, for whatever reason?

With grim irony Sally had heard Sharon say to Sula, 'I don't care what Sally says about her broken engagement not affecting her. She's not herself, and poor Jack's bearing the brunt of it. She's so abrupt with him!'

It wouldn't go on much longer. A locum was coming next week and Jack would be gone… for ever. Sally turned her face to the pillow and tried to choke back the tears that always seemed to be near the surface. Eventually she drifted off into a troubled sleep, waking unrefreshed and late for the Saturday morning surgery.

That afternoon it was the day of the fun fair at the special school. Sally had promised to go, and perhaps it would take her mind off her present troubles. At least it was a sunny, warm day, and she was glad for Ian Kershaw and the staff because she was sure there'd be a good turn-out—there wasn't a lot going on in a little place like Crannoch. Sadly she reflected that she'd wanted to take Jack to the fun fair and show him the good work they did at the school, but although she'd mentioned it to him before, she doubted he would come now.

There were lots of stalls being run by the parents of the children, from coconut shies to a guess-how-many-sweeties-in-a-jar competition.

Sally knew many of the people there and, sure enough, in their jolly company on the sunny afternoon, and despite herself, her spirits began to lift.

She sat down to have a cup of tea and to watch the opening ceremony, which was being performed by Careena Fairfax, the film star who had been affected so badly by the giant hogweed. It was warm and pleasant in the sun and Sally closed her eyes and leant back in her chair, exhausted by emotion and her restless nights. Gradually the murmuring of voices and the little band playing at the other end of the field receded into the background as she relaxed and drifted off to sleep. Then suddenly a hand began shaking her shoulder and, startled, she opened her eyes, confused for a moment as to where she was.

'What on earth…?'

A breathless, panicky voice squeaked, 'Sally! Sally! Please could you come and help? We need a doctor…it's an emergency!'

Sally squinted into the sun to see who it was

and struggled to sit up. 'Why, Sharon, I didn't know you were here…what is it?'

'It's this girl…she's gone into labour.' Sharon's voice was subdued, trying her best to keep the information private. 'I think she's going to have the baby any minute in the tea tent!'

The tea tent! Sally's heart gave a lurch of apprehension. The last time she'd delivered a baby had been a long time ago and it had been in sterile conditions with everything to hand and plenty of professional help. This was going to be a very different experience, she thought wryly as she followed Sharon at a brisk trot.

'Have you rung for an ambulance?' she panted, trying to catch her breath.

'Yes, but it could be some time—there's been a landslide across the main road.'

Sally sighed. Just her luck. It must have been the first landslide for fifty years and it had to happen that afternoon.

'Right, we'll just have to manage, then,' she said with false brightness. She fumbled in her pocket for her mobile phone and hit the buttons. She didn't want to do this—he was the last person she wanted to work closely with now—but if possible, for the sake of the mother and baby, she needed help and medical equipment, and the only help available within five miles was Jack.

'Oh, please,' she breathed, as she waited for Jack to answer. 'Please have your mobile switched on!'

'Yes?' said that deep familiar voice.

She tried to sound composed, but there was underlying tension in her voice. 'Jack, it's Sally. I need you to come to the fun fair at the special school as quickly as you can. Someone's in the throes of having a baby and the ambulance is stuck. Please try and make it. There's no medical equipment here and—'

'I'll be there very soon,' he interrupted calmly. He must have had an inkling of the concern she was feeling because with a hint of humour in his voice he added reassuringly, 'And don't worry, I'll bring my medical bag.'

Thank God he replied, thought Sally gratefully, any thoughts of not wanting to work with Jack disappearing. She felt only intense relief that someone with his skill would be available. Never had his lovely bass voice sounded so welcome.

The young woman was lying on some rugs and cushions on the ground behind one of the trestle tables. Every now and then she gave a deep groan of pain and moved restlessly, clutching the hand of one of the two ladies who'd been serving the tea.

They looked up at Sally with undisguised relief, and one of the women exclaimed, 'Oh, thank goodness you're here, Doctor! We think she's very near her time, poor lamb. We…we weren't sure what to do.' She patted the young woman's hand. 'Don't you worry, you'll be fine now—the professional's arrived,' she said cheerily.

Sally did a quick assessment. The mother-to-be was very pale, dark shadows under her eyes, unkempt looking—and very near delivery, judging by the timing of her groans as she had another contraction.

'Right,' Sally said briskly to the two women. 'Can you find me some clean towels please—

tea towels and hand towels? I'll also need some boiling water.'

The women scuttled off, delighted to be given a task to do. Sally sank down on her knees by the young woman, and soothed back her tangled hair.

'Now,' she said reassuringly, patting the girl's hand, 'I'm going to do my best to help you, and another doctor will be here very soon as well so don't worry. Let's just concentrate on getting this baby born. First of all, what's your name?'

'Nesta…Nesta Grahame…'

Sally was concentrating so hard that she didn't notice Jack coming through the tent entrance. The first she was aware of him was a figure standing beside her.

'At least I'm in time to help,' said Jack.

She kept her voice even, not betraying the startled flutter of excitement she felt at his closeness, but her overwhelming feeling was one of relief that she wouldn't be forced to deliver a baby by herself on the floor of a tea tent!

'Thanks for coming. It shouldn't be long now…things have been moving fast.'

She flicked a look at him and even in these unlikely circumstances she felt the treacherous flutter of attraction flicker through her body. His sexy, drop-dead-handsome looks only re-inforced Sally's realisation of how much she loved him, and how much she was going to miss him when he left, but she wasn't going to show it. Things were over between them. That was what he wanted, wasn't it? His deep blue eyes caught her quick glance and within them was an expression she couldn't easily define. She swallowed hard and forced herself back to the matter in hand.

'This is Nesta.'

Jack looked at the patient and gave an exclamation of surprise.

'But we know each other, don't we? It's Nesta Grahame. You were in the surgery a few days ago and I sent you to hospital. Didn't they keep you in?'

'I discharged myself. They wanted to ask all sorts of stupid questions,' Nesta mumbled. She looked at him, her eyes wide with fright. 'I wish

I hadn't left. I should be in the hospital now. Will…will I be all right?'

Jack gave his old familiar reassuring grin, exuding confidence. 'Of course you will! Dr Lawson and I have worked together many times—we're a great team, aren't we?'

He looked directly up at Sally, and she swallowed and said hollowly, 'Absolutely. We're great at delivering babies.'

'Ahh!' Nesta drew up her knees and gasped as a pain hit her again. Her forehead beaded with perspiration and she clutched Sally's hand in fright. 'It hurts…it hurts so bad… Is something wrong?'

'Nothing's wrong. It's all quite natural. You're doing fine so far,' Sally reassured her.

'What's the time between contractions?' Jack asked.

'About three minutes.'

Jack smiled at Nesta. 'Sounds like you'll have that baby here very soon—he or she's obviously in a hurry. I just want to see if I can see its head and Dr Lawson will listen to its heartbeat.'

The two tea ladies bustled up with a bowl of

hot water as well as towels, which Sally spread under Nesta. Then she took the small foetal Doppler Jack had given her and ran it over Nesta's swollen abdomen. The regular pit-a-pat of a little heartbeat could be heard quite clearly over the background bustle of the fair outside the tent. For a moment Nesta relaxed and gazed in astonishment at the two doctors.

'Is that the baby, then?' She gave a tremulous smile. 'Sounds as if it's running a race.' Then her expression changed suddenly and she sucked in her breath and shouted, 'Oh, God, I can feel it pressing down on me. It's coming right now—I can't stop it!'

'You're right—it's on its way! I can see the head…' Jack's voice was easy, soothing. 'Now, we don't want the baby to come out in a rush. Can you pant a little, then, when I tell you to push, give it all you've got!'

'I can't—I can't do this… Please help me!' Nesta was on the brink of hysteria.

Sally gripped her hand and said firmly, 'You're doing really well—just concentrate on what Dr McLennan tells you to do. I promise you this baby will be here very soon now.'

All of a sudden there was a sudden liquid gush and a slippery little body was propelled into Jack's waiting hands. A few seconds later the baby gave a robust cry. A gasp of awe came from the two tea ladies, who had been standing at a discreet distance, and they clutched each other and dabbed their eyes.

'And it's a little boy,' said Jack softly. 'Congratulations, Nesta!'

Sally was ready with sterile scissors from Jack's bag to cut and clamp the cord. She looked at the expression of mingled happiness and relief on Jack's face at having delivered a healthy baby—and she knew just how he felt. For her it was always an incredibly moving moment to witness the birth of new life and be involved in its arrival, and she knew that Jack felt that too. And in the joy of the moment they grinned happily at each other, forgetting any awkwardness between them. Together they'd helped Nesta bring a baby into the world. Jack wrapped the infant in a towel and handed him carefully to the exhausted mother.

A beatific smile lit up Nesta's face as she held her newborn son. Jack guessed that there hadn't been many truly happy episodes in this young woman's life, but at this moment she was filled with unadulterated joy.

'He's a little belter,' she murmured, looking down tenderly at her baby and stroking his soft cheek. Then she looked directly at Jack, and he knew what she was implying when she said to him, 'Don't you worry, I won't let anyone I know harm him…ever. I'll work it out some-how.' Jack guessed she was making it clear that she would never allow her husband to treat her child as he'd treated her.

'I'm sure you'll not let anyone hurt him, Nesta,' Jack murmured. 'You'll look after him very well.'

The sound of an ambulance's siren floated through to the tent and a minute later two burly paramedics appeared at the entrance. 'Sorry we're late,' one said chirpily. 'Unavoidable, I'm afraid. How far on is the patient's labour? How's she doing?'

'Very well.' Jack grinned. 'She didn't need your help. She's just become the mother of a strapping boy!'

The ambulancemen had borne Nesta and her new baby away. Jack and Sally stood looking at each other, suddenly pitched back into the awkward reality of being together.

'That went well, didn't it?' said Sally lightly. 'Thank you for coming. I...I really appreciated you being here.'

'You'd have managed. You were always good at coping in emergencies.'

Sally didn't want to remember past times and said briskly, 'You'd seen her in the surgery, then?'

He nodded. 'She was brought in after she fainted outside. I guess Nesta has a difficult life. Her husband abuses her and I was worried that this baby might suffer the same fate. Somehow I don't think I've any need to worry. I saw an inner steel there with Nesta—she'll protect her little boy.'

There was silence between them and Sally gazed down at the ground. She felt horribly near to tears. It was so cruel to be so close to Jack and to know that it was over between them— and all because he had this conviction that it would be wrong to inflict himself on her.

'Anyway, thanks again,' she murmured. 'It helps when there's someone you can rely on working with you.'

'We've had a lot of practice.'

They seemed to be mouthing banalities at each other, and suddenly he gave a muttered exclamation, taking a stride towards her and holding her shoulders. He looked down at her wistfully, his dark blue eyes raking her face, tracing a line with his finger across her cheek. He was so close to her—she could feel his breath on her face, smell the faint tang of after-shave, and there was an undercurrent between them of energy and exhilaration after the drama they'd been involved in together.

'Sally…I wish we…' he began, then halted as

if to stop himself saying something he'd regret. He began again rather lamely, 'I'm glad we had this last chance to work together again. It's had a…very happy ending,' he said huskily. He bent his head to hers and brushed her cheek with his lips, and briefly she felt the warmth of his lean, hard body against hers then he turned abruptly and walked out of the tent.

Sally touched her cheek where he had stroked it, her heart thumping against her rib cage. A happy ending? Not for them, she thought in despair, just a tantalising memory of how it had been between them a mere few days ago. But now there was no future in their relationship, nothing to look forward to, and feeling cold and empty she stepped out the tea tent and into the sunshine and the happy noise of the fun fair.

Jack slung his medical bag in the back of his car and stood looking back at the tea tent. Sally had just come out and was standing alone, watching a line of children in fancy dress walking across the field. There was something rather lost and forlorn about her, and Jack's heart went out to her. She'd done nothing wrong, only been mad enough to fall in love with him—and he had let her down yet again.

Seeing her that afternoon, working with her, being so close, had brought back just how much he missed being with her, just how beautiful and sweet she was. After next week he wouldn't see her again and the fleeting resurrection of their old romance would have died down for ever. Jack slammed the car door and slipped the car into gear, driving away quickly and hardly aware that he was gripping the steering-wheel until his knuckles were white.

How close he'd come to happiness, he thought bitterly. Love had blossomed again between them…the future had begun to glow with a happiness he hadn't known for a long time. But when it came to the crunch he was afraid: worried that Sally might regret throwing her lot in with the son of a murderer, and that her parents would be appalled that their precious daughter could be involved in a family like his.

He changed gear noisily, cutting round a corner and scattering some crows pecking at a carcase on the road. Why the hell was he doing this to himself and Sally, denying them both the chance of happiness and allowing his childhood experience with his parents to dominate his life?

Nesta's words after she'd had her baby seemed to echo in his head. 'I'll work something out somehow...' Perhaps he should follow Nesta's example, he thought wryly, and take a leap of faith that, after all, he and Sally had a future. They could overcome anything together.

Suddenly, like a mist clearing in the early morning, he realised what a fool he'd been. Dammit, he and Sally had one life—why should they spend it apart when they loved each other? He looked at the scenery around him and realised that he'd driven almost ten miles down the coast, so deep in thought he'd been. With a mild oath he looked in the mirror and did a U-turn, then drove back to Crannoch. He'd made a decision—he was going to find Sally and tell her he'd made the biggest mistake of his life and they had to get together again. He pressed his foot on the accelerator and drove down the road to the village.

After the fair Sally had decided to go for a brisk walk up the hill behind the cottage and over the fields—it was no good sitting moping at home on a lovely evening. So much had happened to her during the past few weeks that she longed for some space to herself to work things out and think where her future might lie. And she loved this area, she reflected, loved its beauty and tranquillity. She and Jack could have made a good life for themselves here. But being together with him again for probably the last time had only made her feel despair that her life was a series of blunders, always going after the wrong man. Always nearly reaching happiness and then it slipping tantalisingly out of her hands...

She reached the river and leaned for a few minutes against the stone wall that ran alongside it. It was a wide and beautiful stretch of water, meandering peacefully along to the sea, great willows bending above it and trailing their branches along the dappled edges, and something about it soothed and comforted her. She still loved Jack, but she'd get over it, like she had before, and enjoy life once again.

The cracking of a twig behind her made her whip round, and at first she didn't recognise the figure walking towards her against the rays of the evening sun.

'Sally, thank God I've found you...'

She squinted into the light and looked in surprise at Jack standing in front of her. 'What on earth are you doing here?' she said.

'I went to the cottage and a workman told me he'd seen you go off on a walk in this direction. I need to speak to you.'

'Has something happened?'

He stood some way from her and smiled wryly. 'Yes, you could say that...'

'What is it, then?'

'Only that I've come to my senses.' He took her hands and pulled her towards him, gazing down at her bewildered face. 'Oh, sweetheart, what a fool I've been. Happiness was right under my nose and I tried to push it away.'

Sally's expression changed to one of wariness and she snatched her hands away from his. 'I suppose you want us to get together again—is that it? Because, if so, the answer's no!'

He put a finger on her lips to prevent her saying more. 'I don't blame you if you don't believe a word I say but something happened to me this afternoon when we delivered that baby, something that made me realise that we have one life and we have to snatch our happiness when we can.' He tilted her face up to his and said softly, 'I honestly don't think I can live my life without you, Sally, and to hell with my past and the devils in it.'

Sally shook her head impatiently. 'Don't give me all that guff again,' she said wearily. 'You don't want to commit to me and that's all there is to it. I feel sorry for your past—'

'And that's what it is…the past.' He put his hands on her shoulders and she tried to ignore the undeniable sexual attraction that started to flutter through her body. 'I want to look forward—I want to look after you and have babies with you and forget the bad things. I think you still love me, Sally, just as I love you—admit it!'

His eyes were so penetrating, devouring her face as he willed her to confess that she still loved him, and his arm went round her waist and drew her to him. And she didn't resist but stared at him as if trying to decide if this man who had left her twice was really telling her the truth.

'Give me one more chance, sweetheart... please.'

Oh, those blue eyes were so beguiling, pleading with her to believe him!

'I must be mad,' she said at last. 'But it's true—I do love you.'

He looked at her silently for a moment, then buried his face in her sweet-smelling hair. 'Oh, Sally,' he whispered. 'How did I ever deserve you? Could you really take me on—baggage and all?'

And a little bubble of happiness seemed to explode somewhere in the region of Sally's stomach and she suddenly laughed up at him. 'I like a challenge...'

Then before she could say any more, his mouth had found hers and he kissed her hungrily, pulling her down beside him on the soft grassy bank, and she didn't resist when Jack eased off her T-shirt and pulled her against his hard body, his kisses covering her face, her neck and her arms. He feasted his eyes on her rounded curves, his hands moving delicately over her breasts and back, and she forgot entirely that she had told Jack she never wanted to see him again and that she wanted him out of her life.

'For one person you sure have a lot of books,' remarked Sally, as she helped Jack pack his stuff into cardboard boxes.

'Don't you dare throw anything out,' growled Jack. 'Love me, love my books!'

Sally grinned. 'If you're going to move in with me, I'm thinking that my cottage can only take so much stuff—it's going to be a tight squeeze with two of us in it.'

Jack waggled his eyebrows at her. 'Who cares about a tight squeeze? I'm all for it! Anyway, if you think there's any "if" about me moving in with you, please think again. I don't want to live separately from my wife, thank you very much.'

Sally felt the familiar little shock of delight when Jack said 'my wife'—tomorrow they would be getting married in a quiet little ceremony in the tiny church on Hersa. Nobody except Sally's parents and a friend of Jack's knew about it—they both felt that there had been too many dramas and setbacks in their relationship to have a huge public display. It was to be their secret for a day.

Sally gazed lovingly at Jack for a second before going back to putting papers and files into a box and sorting them into some kind of order. She held up a few letters in an elastic band.

'You've some correspondence here. Shall I put it with your other letters in a separate box?' she asked.

Jack glanced at the bundle in her hand and sighed. 'That's part of my past. Perhaps I ought to throw them out.'

'What are they? Are they important?'

He hesitated then said sadly, 'They've no importance now…they're the letters my mother sent me to Australia and I've never read them. Perhaps I should have, but it's too late now. I don't want to read how much she blamed me for the family break-up.'

Sally gazed down at the letters. There were only two of them, slightly faded now. It seemed all wrong that he should never have opened them because his mother had hurt him so much.

'Jack,' she said quietly, 'I think you should open these. You can't just get rid of them without knowing what she had to say to you…and I think you would always regret it if you destroyed them.'

'Nothing she could write could make up for what she put me through,' he said grimly. 'She put my drunken sot of a father before me—I didn't deserve that. I loved her very much, but I don't want to hear her excuses for him.'

Sally went and sat beside him and laid the letters on his lap. 'Please, Jack. You must give her the chance to speak to you through her letters.'

Jack looked down at the envelopes silently, as if willing himself to read them. Then gingerly he picked them up, tore the envelopes open, and began to read their contents. After a few minutes he put the letters back in the box, closed the lid and put his head in his hands. Sally put her arm round him.

'What is it, sweetheart?' she asked softly. 'Is it too painful?'

Jack got up abruptly and strode over to the window, his hands, bunched into tight fists, thrust into his pockets. He gazed out at the shining sea, watching the scudding clouds over Hersa and the little ferry making its way across the sound.

'They're lovely letters,' he said huskily. 'They say how much she loved me and that she didn't hold me responsible for the family break-up. She blames herself for what happened, pandering to my father's drunken behaviour. She thought if she sided with me, all our lives would become unbearable. In a way she was telling me to get as far away from my father as possible.'

'I knew it, Jack! I knew she couldn't have

hated you. I can see that she wanted you to distance yourself from that tragedy and perhaps she felt that was the way to do it—to tell you she didn't want to see you again.'

He turned round and smiled wanly. 'My poor mother,' he said softly. 'Why the hell didn't she leave my father? Staying with him ruined her life…'

Sally got up and put her arms round Jack's waist. 'You know that some women trapped in a marriage they hate find it hard to escape. Your mother lived in a tiny community—perhaps she just couldn't see a way out.'

'Perhaps…' He looked down at the letters in his hand. 'Thank God you made me read them.'

'I think,' said Sally with a smile, 'it's as if she'd given you a special wedding present… think of it like that!'

Jack nodded and smiled at her then suddenly threw the letters up in the air with a whoop of delight as if the full import of it had just hit him. He hugged Sally to him. 'Wow! You're right! It's a gift from Mum and I feel extraordinary, as if a heavy weight's been taken off my shoulders—to know she loved me and didn't really think of me as a traitor.'

Sally laughed, a surge of happiness filling her whole being. It was as if a final piece of a jigsaw puzzle had been put into place and the picture was whole, beautiful. She couldn't wait for the next day, for the simple ceremony that would make Jack and herself man and wife.

'It's going to be perfect, Jack...'

He looked down at her and said softly, 'For six years I've tried to get on with my life without you, my darling, and by some miracle I've found you again. Let's get that champagne out of the fridge and crack it open. Here's to tomorrow—all our tomorrows!'

'And no more secrets?' whispered Sally.

'No more secrets,' he assured her.

The evening was still bathed in the warm glow of sunset as they sailed back from Hersa, scarcely a ripple on the sea, the lights from the ferry flickering on the water, and above them the first few stars beginning to show in the early evening clear sky.

Jack hugged Sally to him. 'We did it—we

did it at last! Can you believe we're actually married?'

Sally sighed. 'It was all wonderful, Jack—like a fairy-tale. I didn't want it to end… Somehow it almost seems an anticlimax to go back to the cottage.'

Jack's blue eyes danced down at her. 'I hope it won't be, my love. I'm sure I can whip up a little excitement somehow!'

The ferry slid up to the jetty and they walked off to where their car was parked. Jack started the engine and drove out of the car park, turning away from the village and up the hill road.

'Why are you going this way?' asked Sally, leaning forward and looking out of the window. 'Isn't it a bit late to go for a drive?'

'I want to show you something,' replied Jack with a secret little grin. 'I think you might be quite interested…'

Sally looked at him sharply. 'I thought there were to be no more secrets, Jack McLennan!'

'This isn't a secret really—it's a surprise. It's a wedding present!'

'A wedding present? Up here?'

Jack nodded but said nothing, just a suppressed look of excitement on his face as he negotiated the bends and twists of the country road.

'This is the way to Hilda Brown's,' said Sally. 'Don't tell me she's ill again.'

The gates of The Chase appeared, and Jack drove through them and up the drive to the beautiful yellow-bricked house. He stopped by the front door and got out of the car, then opened the car door for Sally. She got out and looked at him in bewilderment.

'What's going on?'

Jack felt in his pocket and pulled out a key. 'This is your wedding present, my darling...'

There was a stunned silence then Sally gasped. 'This house? The Chase? You mean you bought it?'

'It was on the open market and I asked Hilda if she'd mind if we put in a bid. She said she'd be delighted...so, you see, there'll be plenty of room for my books...' Jack put his arm round Sally and pulled her close to him. 'What do you think?'

She looked at the lovely house and the shining sea below, with Hersa's hills a blue line in the distance, then back at him with shining eyes. 'Oh, Jack,' she breathed. 'What an end to a perfect day—I can't believe we're going to live here! It's the most beautiful place on earth!'

'And we'll be here, my darling, for many, many happy years.'

Then he opened the door and picked Sally up, carrying her over the threshold and into a brighter future than either of them could ever have dreamed of.

* * * * *

Mills & Boon® Large Print Medical

October

TAMING DR TEMPEST	Meredith Webber
THE DOCTOR AND THE DEBUTANTE	Anne Fraser
THE HONOURABLE MAVERICK	Alison Roberts
THE UNSUNG HERO	Alison Roberts
ST PIRAN'S: THE FIREMAN AND NURSE LOVEDAY	Kate Hardy
FROM BROODING BOSS TO ADORING DAD	Dianne Drake

November

HER LITTLE SECRET	Carol Marinelli
THE DOCTOR'S DAMSEL IN DISTRESS	Janice Lynn
THE TAMING OF DR ALEX DRAYCOTT	Joanna Neil
THE MAN BEHIND THE BADGE	Sharon Archer
ST PIRAN'S: TINY MIRACLE TWINS	Maggie Kingsley
MAVERICK IN THE ER	Jessica Matthews

December

FLIRTING WITH THE SOCIETY DOCTOR	Janice Lynn
WHEN ONE NIGHT ISN'T ENOUGH	Wendy S. Marcus
MELTING THE ARGENTINE DOCTOR'S HEART	Meredith Webber
SMALL TOWN MARRIAGE MIRACLE	Jennifer Taylor
ST PIRAN'S: PRINCE ON THE CHILDREN'S WARD	Sarah Morgan
HARRY ST CLAIR: ROGUE OR DOCTOR?	Fiona McArthur

Mills & Boon® Large Print
Medical

January

February

March

Discover Pure Reading Pleasure with

Visit the Mills & Boon website for all the latest in romance

 Buy all the latest releases, backlist and eBooks

 Find out more about our authors and their books

 Join our community and chat to authors and other readers

 Free online reads from your favourite authors

 Win with our fantastic online competitions

 Sign up for our free monthly eNewsletter

 Tell us what you think by signing up to our reader panel

 Rate and review books with our star system

www.millsandboon.co.uk

 Follow us at twitter.com/millsandboonuk

 Become a fan at facebook.com/romancehq